Stuffed

Miriam Halahmy

To Luke

Happy Reading!

M... H

Albury Fiction

Published in 2014 by Albury Books
Albury Court, Albury, Thame,
Oxfordshire, OX9 2LP
www.alburybooks.com

A CIP catalogue record for this title is available from the British
Library

Printed and bound by CPI Group (UK) Ltd, Croydon, CR0 4YY

ISBN 978-1-909958-73-9 (paperback)

Stuffed

Miriam Halahmy

Albury Fiction

Praise for Hidden

Nominated for the 2012 CILIP Carnegie Medal

Sunday Times Children's Book of the Week

A gripping story...written with clarity and immediacy...this is a book to counter bigotry. — *Nicolette Jones, The Sunday Times*

Hidden is a terrific story. Miriam has managed a rare thing; a serious story told with a comic and emotional touch. — *Anne Cassidy*

Tautly written throughout this fine novel deserves the widest audience. — *Nick Tucker, reviewer and broadcaster*

Miriam left me feeling inspired and empowered to stand up for the things I believe in. Everyone should read this book...It's invigorating. — *The Bookette*

Miriam Halahmy is a truly magnificent author. She makes you think and think. — Phoebe Ridgway. 14 years

Amazing book. I would recommend it to everyone. A real page turner. Go and buy it now. — *Jad Faki. 13 years.*

Praise for Illegal

Excellent! Beautifully written and a really strong and gripping story. — *Wendy Cooling, MBE, co-founder of Bookstart*

Miriam Halahmy has pulled off a difficult trick – a second novel as good as her first. — *Mary Hoffman*

Well written, gritty... an author who can deal with tough, hard-hitting issues and keep things realistic. — *The Bookbag*

Emotional, powerful, addictive. Had me hooked from page one. — *Book Addicted Girl*

A real page-turner... amazing plotline. Never a dull moment. — *Joseph Helm. 10 years.*

Gripping...Miriam's best book so far. — *Matthew. 17 years.*

The Hayling Cycle:

Hidden
Illegal
Stuffed

In loving memory of
Amira Tikva Halahmy
who was a magnet for children all her life.

Chapter 1
Jess

My phone vibrates in my lap. I pick it up and squint at it under the tablecloth. It's Sarah. **Wts up.** Mum frowns at me. She hates me checking my phone when we have guests for lunch. She checks hers all the time of course, when it's just us. I glare at her and put another pea in my mouth.

When Mum turns back to the lunch guests I send a reply. **Nothin. SO borrring here. Call u l8r 2plan.**

Sarah and I have both been single for way too long, so we're going to have a party. I've got an excuse for not having a boyfriend, but Sar's just being picky. She thinks she's going to meet someone on the ski trip, like last year. She pulled the ski instructor, Helmut, in Val d'Isere, then claimed they went out for two months. *I* don't think long distance relationships work, not that Sarah *had* one, but she won't listen. Helmut was twenty-two and totally hot, but all he did was text her a few times. That's not a relationship.

"More chicken, Jessica?" Mum's looming over me with a slice of meat balanced on the serving spoon. It's dripping with gravy. My stomach goes rigid.

Dad's business friends from the Marina, and their wives, are round for Sunday lunch. I realise they've stopped talking and they're all staring at me. Everyone thinks they have the right to watch me eat since I was ill. I hate it.

My sister, Veeve, has a smug grin on her face.

And I snap. It makes me so mad that she's enjoying it, I can't stop myself. "Veeve'll eat it," I say, then mutter, "fatty."

"Mu-um," lets out Veeve, like a six-year-old. "Tell her off!"

"Girls," says Mum in her most disapproving voice, but I know that's all she'll say.

I smirk at Veeve across the table.

My phone vibrates again and Mum takes her chance to put the chicken on my plate. Another text from Sarah. **Lets do facebk page 4 party.** It's time to make my escape.

"I'm going to the bathroom," I say.

Mum frowns again but she gives me a little nod. At least I didn't say "loo". She hates it when we say "loo" in front of guests. I saw Dad slip out of the room without a word about five minutes ago. He's probably making a business call, I think, as I go upstairs. Dad doesn't go on about me eating, he understands. I know he gets distracted by his work a lot, but he's always on my side. He'd tell Veeve off if he heard her being nasty to me.

I don't need the loo, but I couldn't face that plate of food any longer. Ever since I was ill I can't handle eating. I lost so much weight but I hardly ever feel hungry anymore. I still eat, but I know it's not as much as Mum wants me to. I wish she'd just shut up about it though. It's such a relief to get into my room and close the door. I can't ring Sar now in case Mum hears, so I send her a text back. **Yaaay, l8rs x.**

I pull out my diary and curl up on my bed, reading back what I wrote this morning.

sun nov 9
Veeve's getting so fat, even Mum says so. She couldn't get into her old jeans yesterday. She's 3cm shorter than me, even though she's two years older. She takes after Dad. I guess me and Mum are lucky cos we're tall, and we both have naturally good figures. Although now I don't look like I used to at all. Sar says I must be size zero now.

I feel a bit mean having written that, even though Veeve is such a pain. She's not really fat, but next to me she looks obese. She's the shortest girl in the Sixth Form and it shows even if she gains a kilo or two.

There's a noise out on the landing. A footstep. It's probably Mum come to find me. I hide my diary and wait for her to come in. She'll be mad because I didn't go back down to her guests. She'll have a go at me and say, "What will people think?" Mum measures our whole lives by what other people think, really stupid people like the ones downstairs from the Marina. One couple have a hundred-foot ocean-going yacht, but all they do is sit around the Clubhouse at the Marina, drinking cocktails and going on about their condo in Florida.

I listen for movement outside, but I can't hear anything so I get my diary back out.

It will be so amazing to have a boyfriend again. It was Sar's idea to have a party — Sar always has the best ideas. She says she's going to find me a new boyfriend. This is the first term since I was ten that I've been single. Uuuughhhh! I feel so rubbish.

Why does everything bad happen to me? The last four months have been the worst ever. I get so scared my life will never get back to normal. But I can't tell anyone. Not even Sar and she's my best friend....

It makes me feel too sad to read anymore. I close my diary and shove it under the bed. Almost the whole time I was in hospital the doctors didn't even know what was wrong with me, did they? I was absolutely sure I was going to die. And I know Mum and Dad were thinking the same too, only we never talked about it.

Why me? My eyes well up and tears roll down my cheeks. There's too much in my head and it's all too complicated to tell anyone. My diary is the only safe place left to go.

Then I hear that sound again. I brush the tears away, get up and go onto the landing. It's empty. I stop at the stairs and listen, then I crane my neck up to the next floor, where Mum and Dad sleep. There are no footsteps, no creaking doors or flushing loos. I go into Veeve's room, but it's empty.

I wish Dad would come up. He'd see I've been crying and I could have another go at him about signing the letter for the ski trip. There's no way he'd say no with my face all red and smudged. Sarah's Dad has already paid, and someone said even Alix Miller's got a place this year. Alix is poor, so I don't know how they can afford the trip.

I used to think Alix was a loser, but she's all right actually; she's been keeping me up to date with schoolwork because we're in all the same classes. She's still going out with that foreign boy, Samir. *He* can't be going; his family are refugees, even poorer than the Millers. I'm not missing out on the ski trip – I go every year.

Then I hear a different sound, like someone breathing heavily. It's a bit spooky. The bathroom door is open and it looks empty.

I'm just about to call out when I hear rustling in the spare room. Why would anyone be in there? A chill goes through me. What if it's a burglar and I interrupt them stealing something and they attack me? What if they stab me?

The noise stops and there's a horrible silence. I'm only a few steps away. I could tiptoe over and peek in. If there is a burglar, I could scream really loudly and run downstairs. Then Dad would charge up to protect me – he's like that, my Dad. He used to box when he was a kid. Now he just watches it on TV; sometimes he shows us a few moves. He could definitely knock down any burglar.

Feeling all pumped up and ready to scream, I creep up to the open door and peer in.

It isn't a burglar. It's Dad. I go weak with relief. But then I go all cold. He hasn't noticed me; his back's turned, his hair curling over his collar. There's a pile of coats on the bed. They belong to the men downstairs. Dad picks up one of the coats and I start to feel really uncomfortable because from the way he's standing, he looks as though he doesn't want anyone to see him.

I realise I don't want him to know I'm watching either, so all I can do is stand there staring and staring, my eyes aching as though they've popped out of my head, like in a cartoon.

Dad shifts the coat to his left hand and with his right hand he rummages in the pockets. What's he looking for? Maybe one of the men asked him to come up and get their mobile. And sure enough, Dad pulls a Blackberry out of the inside pocket. My legs go weak with relief again.

But then Dad slips the Blackberry back and drops the coat. He picks up another one and his hand goes straight to the inside pocket. This time it isn't a mobile phone Dad takes out. It's a leather wallet, quite a fat one. And Dad doesn't put it straight back. He drops the coat, opens the wallet and starts to pull out a thick wad of banknotes, twenties I think. He shuffles through them quickly, splits the wad in half, then tucks one half back in the wallet and the other half into his back pocket.

I can't help it. A gasp whips out of my throat like a head of steam. Dad turns and our eyes meet.

Chapter 2

I only just reach the toilet in time. I throw up my entire lunch, which wasn't much. Dad taps at the door urgently and says in a low voice, "Let me in, Jess, open the door. I can explain."

Explain what? Why he was going through his friends' wallets? Why he stole a bunch of notes from one? Why he was sneaking around upstairs and scaring the life out of me?

The words "common thief" run through my mind. That's what Mum called one of the girls in Veeve's art class who was caught shoplifting. And now my Dad is a common thief. It makes me feel sick to think of it. My Dad ... a thief ... stealing.... The words go round and round in my head.

Dad taps on the door again, pleading now, "Come on, Jess, before someone comes, let me in."

What if someone does come upstairs? What would we say? I feel as though I'm going to suffocate. You can die from vomiting, can't you?

But I can't die, not after everything else that's happened to me. All that time in hospital, all the tests, the fear, the doctors and those horrible machines. At night when I'm in bed I can still hear them beeping. Sometimes I even think I can feel the lumps in my neck.

I get to my feet, run the cold tap in the sink, take a long drink and splash my cheeks with water. I dry my face and catch sight of myself in the mirror. I'm shocked at how pale and red-eyed I look. Even in hospital, I didn't look this bad.

I unlock the bathroom door and stand back. Dad comes in quickly and shuts the door behind him. He looks like a burglar, all furtive and shady. I've never seen him like this. It completely freaks me out. Maybe he's always been like this; maybe I just haven't noticed before.

"Jessie, darling, just listen to me, please," he whispers, glancing over his shoulder. "It's not like it looks. It's just a loan."

"So they know you took that money?"

"Not exactly...."

"So you stole it?"

Saying that makes me feel sick again. This is all so wrong. It's really weird standing so close to Dad in the bathroom, the smell of toilet cleaner mingling with his aftershave. Dad's forehead is damp and his eyes are panicky.

"It's been a hard year," he says in a breathless voice. I feel as though he's pleading with me. He rushes on. "The business isn't doing so well—"

"But *we're* all right?" I don't understand. We're loaded. Dad's loaded.

"Well, we were. But things are different now, Jessie."

"You were going to sign the skiing letter this weekend, now I'm getting better."

"I'm sorry. Things have changed. You can't tell anyone, Jessie."

He's still talking in that pleading tone. It's making my skin crawl.

"I don't know what....", he stops and rubs his face with his hands, "... the money is all gone." He stops abruptly, his hands drop to his side and his head hangs down.

8

Gone? What does he mean?

He doesn't look like my Dad anymore. Big, funny, confident Dad, who's always on my side, who spoils me rotten, especially when I was ill, bringing me anything I asked for.

How long has this been going on? I think about the skiing letter. How long have I been nagging him to sign it and give me the cheque for the deposit? It's been ages now, and he keeps giving me some excuse. I can't believe I didn't realise something was wrong. But why would I? Dad always sorts everything out. I feel so stupid. First he said I wasn't well enough yet, which I guess makes sense, but last week he told me he couldn't find the cheque book. I wasn't even worried; I just thought he'd sort it out, like he always does.

I feel dizzy and I want to run away from him or shout at him, but I force myself to listen.

"The thing is, Jess, the firm's gone bust. The new development at Southsea hasn't sold; everything hinged on that this year and the banks won't lend anymore. It all happened so quickly. We took a couple of risks a while ago and it's spiralled out of control. Our Director, Anthony Perrins, is the main investor and even he can't bail us out."

His voice falters and I'm standing there staring at him. His expression is so twisted and unfamiliar, it feels like I'm looking at a stranger.

"But what about our savings? What about the shares?" I don't really know anything about my family's money, but I know we have shares in the company.

"All our savings were in the company, Jessie. The shares

are worth nothing. The company's gone down completely. There's nothing left."

Nothing. How can there be *nothing*? Mum did a huge shop today for lunch and she gave Veeve twenty quid for her school outing to the theatre.

"So you stole? From your friends?"

"It's not like that," Dad says, looking shocked. "I'll pay it all back, Jessie. They won't notice a few quid missing; they never know what's in their wallets. I don't normally have a clue myself."

This is insane. Dad really thinks this is OK. He's got to put it back. Then we can go downstairs and everything will go back to how it was. The Marina lot will leave and I'll go over to Sarah's and everything will be all right.

"Put it back," I say defiantly.

"I just need to pay a couple of bills. It's just a few quid, Jess. Give me a chance to put things right."

Dad throws a nervous glance towards the door.

"They'll be wondering where we are. Jess, please don't say anything. I'll put it right, I promise, but if you go down and tell *anyone....*" He says that last word so viciously I jerk back, surprised. Our eyes meet. For a second he looks a bit like a dog about to attack. His teeth are bared, his eyes narrowed, his breathing rapid. I feel quite scared, which is mad. This is my Dad! "Think how your mother would feel if she found out!"

I get a sudden vision of Mum sobbing in front of "the girls" from the Marina – who she always meets up with at the Clubhouse – her mascara running down her face, trying to hide her embarrassment. Imagine what it would be like to come from a family of criminals. Lindy Bellows from school does. She's got two brothers in prison. They're always in trouble, her family. And she doesn't even seem ashamed.

But my family, criminals? No way. We're not like that. My dad has a job and he works hard so we have all the things we do. He works for a living and that's why we go on nice holidays, because we deserve a break somewhere hot. Sarah's family are well off too. Me and Sarah and Emily all went around together before Emily left. We were the Jayne family, putting Jayne after all our names. I was Jess Jayne, the leader, and everyone was jealous of us. I just want everything to go back to normal.

I want to yell all this at Dad as we stand there in the bathroom, but my throat has closed up and tears well up in my eyes.

"It's a secret, Jess, just between us!" Dad's almost hissing at me. "Until I get back on my feet. It won't be long, I promise you. But you must keep this a secret from Mum and Veeve, OK Jessie? OK?"

Secret? What was it they were always telling us in junior school? If an adult makes you do anything you don't like, tell someone, your teacher or your Mum.

Who can I tell this secret to?

I feel trapped. I push past Dad and run to my room. I close the door behind me with as much restraint as I can, so no one hears, and throw myself on the bed, burying my face

11

in the pillow to muffle the great big gushing sobs, which I can't hold back any longer.

I usually make the most noise possible when I cry, so that Dad comes running to me. But I don't want anyone to come near me now. After a long time, I reach under my bed for my diary – the only safe place left in all the world.

Chapter 3

"Pass the salt, Jess," Dad says.

It's Monday breakfast. I look round the table at my family. I've been awake all night going over and over it in my mind. Why does Dad look as though nothing's happened? Why don't I tell Mum and Veeve now what I saw and get it over with? Only the memory of Dad's voice hissing in the bathroom – "Think how your mother would feel" – stops me.

Mum's got her Monday outfit on, black leggings and a crop top. Her tummy is as flat as mine. It's Legs, Bums and Tums at the Clubhouse today, and she's meeting the girls for lunch. She's got her light brown hair pulled back in a scrunchy, and I can see her eyebrows need threading but I don't say anything.

Veeve's slapping on her makeup. They wear what they want in the Sixth Form, but she looks fat in the top she's wearing. She's got the same hair colour as Mum. Mine's darker, like Dad's side of the family. But we've all got brown eyes.

"Jess?" says Mum in an irritated voice.

"What?"

"Your father wants the salt."

I don't answer.

Mum reaches over and pushes the salt towards me. I pick it up and I'm about to pass it to Dad when a surge of anger rises up through me and I sort of slam it down in front of him. The table shakes and his black coffee spills onto the white tablecloth. Our eyes meet and he shoots me a wary look, but he doesn't say anything.

Go on, I think, I dare you. Tell them, just tell them.

"For heaven's sake." Mum glares at me.

"What?" I say, still staring at Dad.

But he looks down at his plate and his ears are going pink. Embarrassed, angry, ashamed? Does he care about yesterday? Maybe he thinks I've forgotten all about it overnight and I'm just in a mood.

"Ronny?" says Mum.

Dad shrugs and butters a slice of toast.

"Aren't you going to say something to your daughter?" She's got a telling-off tone on, cold as an ice cube.

"She's got so spoilt since she was ill," mutters Veeve. "So demanding."

"Jealous Genevieve," I snap back. She hates it when we use her full name. And I am so ready for a row. I want to scream and shout and smash all the crockery. Anything to let out this pain inside me and let Dad see what he's doing to me.

"You milked it," Veeve says in a low voice.

"I was ill, in case you didn't notice. Stupid cow."

"Jessica!" Mum snaps but her phone bleeps. It's a text from one of the girls. She picks up her phone, mutters, "Oh not again, Angela," gives a little giggle and starts texting back.

"A Pandora bracelet," Veeve says, "Jimmy Choo boots, those expensive spirit ink pens – *for my coursework, Daddy,*" she puts on a mocking voice.

"Maybe you should try *dying* sometime," I say.

14

"You weren't dying."

"I was on a cancer ward! I thought I was dying, and so did all of you!" I'm almost screaming.

Dad is staring at his plate. Veeve smirks at me and goes back to her mirror to renew her lip gloss. She's pleased to have riled me. Mum's giggling and shaking her head at her phone. I feel as though I'm in a room full of strangers, and for a moment I honestly wonder whether I was adopted.

Last term, one of the girls at school found out she'd been adopted. Her family had kept it quiet for fifteen years. Her brother found the papers and stuck them to her door with a dart. She took an overdose. She had to have her stomach pumped out, and the father beat up the brother.

Then Mum clicks off her phone and glares at me. Her giggly phone voice switches back to her telling-off voice. "Jessica, darling, of course we were all worried about you. It was a terrible time, very frightening for all the family, and we know you still have a lot of hospital appointments – they have to make sure they haven't missed anything, don't they?" She lowers her voice into freezer mode, "But that's no reason for you to behave like this to your Dad!"

"She's such a drama queen," says Veeve, peering into her mirror.

"And your point is?" I snap back.

"All I'm saying is, I don't see why you're being so nasty to Dad when he gave you everything you wanted. I got nothing."

Veeve's always going on about all the stuff I got. I'm sick of hearing it. She would have done the same, worse probably.

She's right, of course. When it all started I did get what I could out of Dad.

I was so ill and scared and tired, with lumps in my throat, and it went on all summer. I missed all the beach parties and shopping trips to London. All I had was hospital appointments and tests.

The only way I could keep in touch with my friends was on Facebook.

Jess Jayne Fitzgerald im sick sick sick of needles
Like • Comment • Share
Sarah Jayne Lewis tell them u want botox ☹
Hello Kitty aww hunii
Karl Reece have you had a second opinion?
Alix Miller im photocopying history notes for you ☺

The weirdest thing was that when I went into hospital in September, Mum turned into Florence Nightingale. Unbelievable. She didn't seem that interested in us when we were little. We weren't minted then and she worked as a hairdresser. She had a string of sitters for us, and went out all the time.

Then I got ill, and suddenly she was in total nursing mode and Dad was always disappearing. He'd hover at the end of my bed for a few minutes, mutter that he had a big project on at work and then he'd take off.

I thought he didn't like me anymore because I was so sick and thin and ill. I'd always been his apprentice, his trainee, hadn't I? He used to say, "You're hungry for money, Jessie, like me. You'll get on, not like Veeve with her arty farty crowd." But now I know why he wasn't around when I was in hospital. It wasn't my illness. Dad was losing all his money. If anyone on this planet is hungry for money, it's my Dad.

"It's only a bit of coffee, no harm done," says Dad now, and he's sprinkling salt on his scrambled egg. There's something about the jaunty way he's doing it, waving his hand up and down like he always does, as if he hasn't a care in the world, which sends me wild.

"Harm!" I yell. "What do you know abou—?"

"That's enough Jess, get ready for school," snaps Mum.

I'm glaring at Dad but he won't meet my eyes. Surely he's going to tell them what's happening? He can't let them think this is all down to me.

But he doesn't say anything.

Veeve and Mum exchange looks and Veeve says, "Ground her."

Mum adjusts her hair with a sharp tweak, as though she agrees. Dad takes a bite of toast.

I'm close to tears and I don't want them to see. Just like I couldn't slam my door last night, I have to keep Dad's secret and give him a chance to put things right. Then Mum won't need to know and we can just forget about everything and get back to normal.

I stand up too quickly and I jog the table quite hard. A big slurp of coffee spills out, spraying everything.

"That's it...." Mum starts, but I'm gone. I run out of

the kitchen and down the hall. I rip my coat off the hall peg, pick up my bag, pray I have my bus pass and go out, slamming the door behind me.

As I walk down the road to the bus stop my phone goes. It's Dad. His voice is quite low – maybe he's in the downstairs loo so Mum and Veeve can't hear him.

"Jessie, sorry darling, just give me a bit of time. I'll sort it, I promise. Please don't blow this and tell your mum. You know how badly she takes things when they don't go to plan. OK? OK, Jess?"

I feel so scared of doing something to make things worse and I'm in tears now, so I say, "Hurry up, Dad, please, I can't stand this."

His phone goes off. Mum must be nearby and so he can't answer me.

How can this be happening? My Dad's always making me laugh and spoiling me. It's always been me and Dad, Mum and Veeve. He's been training me to take over the business since I was twelve. That's why I chose Business Studies in school. He even lets me borrow his credit card to go shopping, because he knows I won't forget the pin number or lose it. Not like Veeve, even though I'm fifteen – well, nearly sixteen – and she's eighteen.

I don't want to go to school. I can't face everyone. Sar will guess I've been crying, and I don't know what to tell her. I've already fallen so far behind since I was ill. Coursework's piling up and there are test questions being set all the time.

What's the point? I might as well leave now. I mean, if

Dad's lost all his money I can't go to uni and do Business anymore. And Veeve's got a place at Art School for next year. She won't be able to go either.

A mean little flutter goes up through me as I think of her face when he tells her. But I end up just feeling really miserable. I can't go to school and I don't want to go back home.

There's only one person I can go to now. Nana Hat.

Chapter 4
Ryan

Wednesdays are one of my best days: it's almost the weekend; I finish one hour early, which is the hospital's way of saying you work flexi-time; and Mum does a mid-week roast. Well, chicken legs, but you also get roast potatoes, Yorkshire pudding and peas.

Eleven is usually the slow time before the end of clinic rush, and I'm just checking the football results when this girl comes up to the desk. She's not crying but she looks like she could.

I wait for her to say something and then I can see she's not going to, so I say, "Got your appointment card?"

She shakes her head and mumbles, "Sorry."

"That's OK," I say. "Just give me your name, I'll find you on the system."

"Jessica Fitzgerald."

Nice name. She's got all her hair, but she's thin. Recovering maybe, or undiagnosed. I tap her name into the computer. She's due a scan today and she's two hours late. She's all nervous, looking over her shoulder and fumbling for a tissue in her pocket. I move things about a bit on the appointments sheet and say, "You can go next."

That was worth it, because she gives me a titchy smile. She's very pretty.

She turns to go in this weary way I've noticed the long-term sick have. She knows the routine and she hates it. So I call out in a cheery voice, "See you when you come out."

She doesn't turn round but her head tips slightly to one side. *You're in there, Ryan, mate*, I can almost hear Max whisper in my ear. But Max doesn't get sweaty hands when he pulls.

It suddenly gets busy and the queue stretches out the door. One of the patients is blind drunk, and an old woman with a shopping trolley moans on about her transport coming late again. When Jessica Fitzgerald comes out of Imaging I almost miss her. She's got her head down and she's trying to get to the door but the queue of people are in the way. She's so gorgeous, and I know Max wouldn't let her go without saying something. I have to make a move before she's gone.

"Hey, let's have a bit of space here," I say.

I go over to the queue, rearrange the drunk and the whining lady with the shopping trolley and carve a gap to the door. Jessica Fitzgerald gives me a tiny glance and a nod of thanks as I push the door open and she goes through. Suddenly we're on the other side, in the corridor. It's really quiet and it's just us. She stops, as if uncertain which way to go, and I do it, I grab my chance to pull.

"Got a break coming up, do you want a coffee?"

She stares down the corridor and I think I've blown it. She thinks I work for the enemy, all the doctors and scanners and students poking round her privates. You're dumb, Ryan, you've always been dumb.

"OK, Starbucks in five," she says, and she's gone.

I'm left in the corridor with my mouth open, gaping at

her narrow back and long, long legs, her shoulders humped over as she walks away.

It takes a bit longer than five minutes to get Shelley to agree to let me have a break and then I'm swinging down the stairs and out of the main entrance to the Starbucks on the High Street. She's sitting there with an iPhone in her hand and a hot chocolate in a take-away cup.

"Hey," I say, standing over her.

"Hey," she says back and there's a bit of a smile.

"You want another?" I nod to the cup, which is really dumb because it's full.

She shakes her head, gripping the phone as if she's on the Titanic and it's her lifeline.

I go up to the counter and get a coffee, which seems to take forever. Finally I come back and sit down, holding the cup nervously in both hands. She's still looking at her iPhone and doesn't look at me.

"On Facebook?" I ask, for something to say. I don't do the Internet; I'm on the computer enough at work. When I get home I want to feel a spanner in my hand, not a mouse.

She shakes her head. "Doesn't seem to be working today. Maybe Dad cancelled the contract."

There's a silence. Say something, I think.

"I'm Ryan." I hold out my hand, which then feels completely dumb. I pull it straight back and mutter, "I know your name already."

But she puts the iPhone down and says, "I'm Jess."

Right, OK, I think, I can do this.

"Er, do you live round here?" Max wouldn't ask that! He'd ask her about the apps on her phone or something else cool. But Jessica Fitzgerald – Jess – answers me.

"I live on Hayling Island. Near the golf club."

Oh God, I know exactly where that is, she's loaded. Her Dad's probably a city banker. I wipe my sweaty hands on my jeans and she takes a sip of her chocolate. The Beatles are pumping out over the music system and I can't think of anything to say except, "Do you want to be my girlfriend," and I can't say that, can I?

"Are you at the clinic every day?" she asks, and she sounds like she's being polite, which makes me feel even more nervous.

"Yes, no, I mean, now I am, this week anyhow. Before I was in Orthopaedics."

She doesn't respond; she just picks up her iPhone and starts tapping really fast.

I get my phone out and try to think of a way of asking for her number. But I'm sort of staring at her too. Her face looks like it's been carved in plaster; it's very, very pale. Her hair is long and shiny. She spends a lot of time in front of the mirror, I decide.

Only she's been sick, hasn't she? Really sick. Her file says she's been coming here since August, and that she's had a million tests and even been in hospital on a cancer ward. Scary. But Jessica Fitzgerald hasn't got cancer. She's got sarcoid. It's very rare but it doesn't kill you, just takes you a long time to get better. She must have got one hell of a fright. I can't see her whole file, and I think now I've read it that I probably shouldn't have read what I did. I'm not sure if I'm even allowed to ask patients out.

"So why would your Dad cancel your phone?" I ask. The minute it comes out, I'm sorry.

Her face clouds over and her shoulders slump a bit and she just mutters, "Parents."

"Yeah, right," I say quickly, even though my Mum and Dad are basically OK.

She's fiddling about with the iPhone, as if she can get it to work again just by tapping on it. I fiddle with my phone too. I want to talk to her, but I can't think of anything to say.

She finally looks up and says, "What's ortho-whatsits?"

I'm just about to explain when Olu, one of the hospital porters, shows up.

"Hey Ryan, man. You in plenty trouble now. Shelley yelling for you all over. You better leave the nice lady, man, and come back quick." Olu gives Jessica his big white-teeth grin.

Jess jumps to her feet, mutters something about being late, and she's gone. I didn't even get her number.

I race back, but only because I want to check the computer and find out when she's next in for a scan.

Shelley has me running files around all afternoon, and by the time the shift ends I haven't had a chance to get back on the computer.

I just want to be on my own when I get home, and think up a plan for getting Jessica Fitzgerald's phone number. But Mum's onto me the minute I get through the front door.

"Come back here, Ryan, I want to speak to you."

"Oh, Mum!"

I'm halfway up the stairs and James is coming down. He shoves past me and says with a sneer, "*Oh, Mum!*" Mum starts going on and on about tidying the garage, like she does most days, "... and there's grease spots on the lino floor. You know what I've said about grease in the kitchen."

"Sorry, Mum, I'll get them off, promise. I'm just going upstairs, just for a sec."

She can read me like a book, which annoys me but it's useful sometimes. She stares up at me for a second and then says quietly, "All right love, but dinner's nearly ready," and she goes off, yelling at James to set the table.

Dinner's a nightmare. James has found a picture of Morocco I tore out of a magazine. He holds it up, laughing. "What a dump, who'd want to go there," he says, as he spears the last chicken leg.

"That's where Africa starts," says Dad, and I nod.

Dad's on my side. He's helping me get the camper van ready for my road trip to Africa, and I love working on the van with him.

Mum's so worried about the trip that I try not to talk about it much in front of her. But James keeps on bringing it up. He just turned fourteen, and if he doesn't watch it he won't make it to fifteen.

"Snakes." says James in a smug voice. "Think of Africa and you think of snakes."

I feel my palms go sweaty again. He threw a grass snake at me last week and I screamed like a girl. He'll never let me live it down.

25

But it's not a real phobia until it stops you doing stuff, is it? Like that woman I saw on telly who had a phobia about buttons and couldn't ever do any washing. I'm going to Africa, and I'm not changing my mind now. If the van breaks down on the way, I'll fix it as I go. That's what I love doing, really.

"You won't get snakes in the van, love, will you?" says Mum in her worried voice. "I don't know why you can't go to Norway – nice clean country and they don't have anything dangerous. It's like Britain."

"Exactly why it's got to be Africa," I say, but basically, I'm terrified. Maybe you can get a spray against snakes, like you can against mosquitoes and flies. I'll ask Max next time I'm in the camping shop....

"No such thing as snake-proof vans; and I laid the table so you're washing up," says James as he leaves the room. "Got a Maths exam tomorrow."

"Good boy. Make sure you don't study too late, you need your sleep," Mum calls after him.

Me and Dad exchange looks.

I don't get to be on my own for another hour. Dad wants to show me this new socket set he's got for me, and I have to clean the lino in the kitchen. But then I'm lying on my bed listening to music, and I'm thinking of a hundred ways I can get Jessica Fitzgerald to go out with me.

All of them are completely dumb ideas. James would just ask her, wouldn't he?

Wouldn't think I was the big brother here.

Chapter 5

I have to wait until Friday afternoon before I see Jessica Fitzgerald again. But then she's here, right in front of me, as I'm searching through files on the computer.

"Hey," she says.

I just stare at her and realise my mouth is hanging open. "Hey," I say, but it comes out like a sort of croak. I can't think of anything else, even though I've gone over it a hundred times in my head.

"X-ray," she says with a shrug. She's still carrying her iPhone.

"Oh, right," I say, and look it up on the computer.

Ask her, man, just ask her, I'm yelling at myself. But the words won't come out. She's staring at her nails and her fingers look so pale, almost see-through. Whatever this illness was, it certainly leeched the blood out of her.

"So is that back on?" I ask, and she stares at me.

"Sorry?"

"The phone," I say, going all hot. I remember she got upset before, something about her Dad. Maybe she thinks I'm having a go at him. "I'm sure you could persuade your Dad...." My voice trails off and she looks away.

"Not *this* time."

She looks so sad that I take my chance and blurt out, "Doing anything tomorrow? Would you like to go for a walk? On the beach or ... somewhere...."

A man comes up, all moustache and leather jacket,

27

waving a card in my face and saying, "How much longer? I've got a meeting at four."

I have to deal with him, and Jessica Fitzgerald moves off and takes a seat.

After a while they call her for X-ray and Shelley comes up and gives me an earful about the new spreadsheet system, which she hates. I think I've missed Jess, but then I see her hanging around at the end of the counter.

"Need another appointment?" I ask.

"Meet at the chip shop at two tomorrow?" she says.

I nod and she's gone.

Awesome.

I tell Max when I go in the camping shop on Saturday morning.

He reckons I'm mad. "Going out with a sicko? What's she got, AIDS?"

"Mate, that's confidential. But it's nothing infectious and she's gorgeous."

I don't add, "And she said yes." Who cares if she's sick? She's recovering, isn't she? I don't exactly ask girls out all the time. Jessica Fitzgerald said yes and she's really beautiful, that'll do me. Max is snorting as he rifles through a tray of tent spikes on the counter. "Where're you taking her?"

"Fish and chips on the beach."

Max is an outdoors man, goes off climbing mountains and wrestling with the elements most weekends. He's totally obsessed with climbing Everest, so he won't come with me to Africa.

He works in his Dad's camping shop on the High Street.

They nearly went under this year so they started a sideline in coffee and sandwiches, undercutting the chains. You can sit in a tent at a little camping table, drinking instant out of a tin mug for 50p. It's quite popular.

"You'll freeze your bums off," says Max, coiling a length of rope.

"I'll wrap up warm, *Mum*."

He laughs and shakes his head. He keeps his red hair shaved down to a grade one, but he always wears a black beanie.

Max has got a climber's body – at least that's what he's always telling everyone. He's got really long, thin legs and his feet are so sensitive he can almost see with them, every tiny crack and foothold.

"There are climbs in North Wales that are tougher than anything you'd get on Everest," he told me once.

His fingers are long and thin too. He can send them all over the rock like Spiderman sensing the grooves and cracks.

"Three points of contact at all times, that's the climber's rule," he says. "Only move one hand or one foot, never two together. Once you lose your three points, you're a goner."

His Dad used to climb until a mate slipped beneath him and was killed in the Alps.

"When I started," Max said, "I didn't tell Dad for a year. But he's cool with it. He knows I have to. I can't help it. It's in the blood, man."

I'm shorter than Max and my hair grows like mad in sort of curls – "Like a girl," James sneers in front of everyone. I don't know what's in my blood. Engine oil I think, and now I've decided to go on my road trip, I suppose travel's in my blood. But I wish Max was going with me; he's brave, has to be to climb.

"Everyone falls," he says in a low voice so his Dad doesn't hear. "You just get up and do it again. There's nothing like climbing. It's a proper legal high."

I'm not brave; I just want something that's not the hospital, or Shelley screaming in my ear.

When I get to the chip shop Jess is already there. I feel flustered and say, "Sorry I'm late, haven't got my wheels at the moment."

She shrugs and says, "You're OK."

She's wearing a little purple skirt over leggings. She's got a padded jacket with a furry hood on, but she looks cold.

"Cod or haddock?" I say, and she stares at me.

I stare back.

"Sorry?" she says.

She seems to say that a lot. She's got a scared look about her but not a look of someone who's dying, more a look of someone who's been hurt. Am I the rebound date?

"The fish ... cod or haddock?" I say.

There's an embarrassing silence. She stares at me again as if she doesn't recognise me. I think she's going to make some excuse and leave again, but she says, "Cod."

"Salt and vinegar?" asks the guy serving. The queue is building up behind us and Jessica Fitzgerald is standing with her shoulders hunched, hood up as if we're already in the teeth of a winter gale.

I nod, hand over a tenner, pocket the change and grab

the bag with the food in it. "Let's go," I say, a bit abruptly, and she jerks into life and heads out the door.

"Beach?" She nods again.

So we cross the road and walk through the little car park and the gap in the wall.

The beach is straight and wide along this part of the Island and at low tide there used to be great stretches of sand. But they brought in truckloads of stones because everything was washing into the sea, and so now the beach is covered with pebbles. You can see right across the Solent to the Isle of Wight. It's a really windy day and there are dozens of yachts tacking across the water.

She seems to relax a bit when we get off the road. We sit down and she opens her fish and chips but she doesn't start eating. I'm starving, and as I pick up a chip I say, "You doing A-Levels?"

"Next year, maybe."

"Thinking of leaving?"

She doesn't answer but there's a really sad look on her face so I say, "I'm just working temporary 'til I go on my road trip."

"Where?" she asks, and her eyes sort of light up a bit.

"Africa."

"That would be so cool," she says in a sort of dreamy voice, "to drive far away."

"Yeah. Do you want to travel?"

But she doesn't answer this time. So I eat my fish and chips and she picks at her food and the waves swish over the pebbles, leaving behind all the rubbish from the other side of the world.

I bought the camper just after last Christmas. Dad helped out and it was cheap, got it from a family over at West Wittering. It's done a hundred thousand miles and it's a bit old and battered. Smelt of dead rat at first. They had it in a garage for two years.

James makes farting noises whenever he sees it.

I don't care what it smells like. It's got a little sink and a seat that turns into a bed. Dad's helping me do it up and then I'm off. I'm going to load it up with Diesel jeans, well, fakes from the market, and flog them to pay my way. Olu, who's from Nigeria, gave me the idea.

"You can do very well, Ryan, man, in Africa," he'd said. "Africans, they want western things and they will pay. Go to the universities and stand around with your jeans. They will buy them, oh yes." And he'd shaken his right hand as if something was stuck to it and grinned.

Olu shouldn't be here; he's here illegally, but no one's spotted him yet.

"I know how to hide, man, they won't catch me," he said.

"Yeah, but what if they do?"

"Then I go home and work on my father's farm. Come again next year."

He doesn't seem too bothered; he's seeing the world, like I will be, I guess. But I'll make sure I've got the right visas to travel. Don't fancy the inside of an African prison. Olu has seen one of those too, and his descriptions of the toilets are enough to make me want to stay home.

I've told everyone I'm going now, so I can't cry off, can I? Just because I'm scared of the bogs, or snakes.

"I've had enough," Jess says, breaking into my daydreams. She's throwing the rest of her food, which looks like most of it, to the gulls. They're dive-bombing to catch it in their beaks. Max calls them rats of the sky.

"I don't feel much like eating since I've been ill," says Jess as she catches me looking at her. "Everyone keeps nagging me to put on weight."

I don't know what to say so I break off a bit of fish and chuck it upwards. It turns into a competition, who can get the most gulls. When we only have one chip left each, she wins, feeding the last gull, and we jump up at the same time and she breaks into a laugh.

"Let's walk," I say, and we go down to the water's edge.

The tide is out and there's a good stretch of firm sand. Her foot catches on a pebble and she stumbles. I grab her wrist to stop her falling and she doesn't shake me off.

Her wrist is very thin; I can feel all the bones in it. We're walking and I take her hand almost without realising it. It feels very soft and light. We don't look at each other or say anything.

We'll walk all the way to the funfair, I decide, holding hands.

Then a voice calls out, "Jess!"

It's a big blond guy, expensive jacket, white jeans, higher up the pebble breakwater. He comes slithering down and Jess's face lights up a little bit again. She lets go of my hand sort of quickly. They hug. I stand there like a spare part.

"Hi, Scott. What are you doing here?" Her voice is

different, more alive. Is this the guy who dumped her?

He glances over at me. "All right?" he says with a nod and then he says to Jess, "Meeting Paige." He gives Jess a quick grin and she gives a little smile back but her shoulders have drooped a bit.

"Going to the Hut," says this Scott bloke, punching into his mobile. "You coming?" He gives me a hard stare and I look away.

The Hut is a coffee place that the Park Road High School crowd hang out in. It's for kids. Me and Max go to the pub.

Jess's face shuts down again; she's got the sad 'sorry' look back and she mutters, "Maybe another time."

"Whatever," he says, and you can see he's full of it, all puffed up – the type with girls hanging on his every word.

There's the honk of a horn on the road above us. A couple of blokes in a red convertible have just pulled up.

He says to Jess, "Later," gives me another nod and he's off, striding up the beach, phone to his ear.

Jess stares after him, her hands hanging loose by her side. Then she turns and flicks her hair back. "Scott Fellows," she says.

"Oh," I say.

"I know him from school," she says, staring out to sea as if she's searching for something on the horizon that doesn't seem to be me.

So, I'm second best aren't I? Scott Fellows is one of those cocky blokes, like James, who can pull and pull and pull.

Max was right. Should have left Jessica Fitzgerald behind at work on the computer.

But then Jess turns and smiles at me and says, "Walk a bit?", and I burst inside.

Chapter 6
Jess

It's cold on the beach and Ryan asks me if I want to meet him later, go to the pub. He's too old to hang out in the Hut with the kids from school.

"I have to visit my Nana," I say. It sounds like an excuse but it isn't, it's an emergency. Anyway, I'm too tired to go out all evening but I don't want to say. Not very sexy, is it?

"Oh, right." He looks a bit downcast but he shrugs and says, "Got to do some work on my van anyway. I'm leaving just after Christmas and you know...."

"Only six shopping weeks," I mutter, and then there doesn't seem to be anything else to say.

We walk back up to the main road and my bus pulls up. I give him a quick peck on the cheek, call out, "Thanks for the chips," and jump on the bus.

Will I be single forever? I think as I watch Ryan walk off, his hands in his pockets, shoulders hunched over.

I get off the bus at the top of the Island. Nana Hat lives in a flat for old people near the oyster beds, my favourite place on the Island. When Nana could walk better we used to go and sit on a bench and she would name all the birds for me. The oyster beds don't have any oysters now, they're like nature reserves.

Stuffed

"Second visit this week, lovey, I'm popular," says Nana when she sees me.

She means when I came round on Monday morning after the row at breakfast. She doesn't know what's going on at home of course. Right now I feel like she's the only person in the world who cares about me.

Nana Hat is my great grandma, Dad's grandma. Her real name is Harriet, but everyone calls her Hat, even though she hates wearing hats. "Plasters me hair down, don't they!" she's always saying.

She brought Dad up from the age of five. His Dad, Nana's son, died in a pub fight when he was twenty-six. Dad's Mum got some awful illness the following year and she died too. He hardly remembers his parents. We all love Nana Hat; she's like everyone's grandma. Even Sarah calls her Nana Hat.

"I can't stay long," I say.

I'm really tired after walking on the beach, and from this horrible week. I want to curl up in bed with my iPod. But I'm desperate for a phone that works.

Nana bangs her Zimmer frame into the skirting board as she turns slowly, bent over. It looks like they've just done her hair. It's all snowy and white and nicely fluffed around her cheeks. She's got the family's brown eyes.

"So, what can I do you for, lovey?" she says as she sits down in her special chair. She's wearing the mauve and pink cardigan we bought her for Mother's Day, and I want to hug her and cry and tell her all about Dad.

37

But she's so small, so very, very small. A bad shock could blow her away. If I tell her what Dad's been up to it might give her a heart attack. It's such a horrible thought I feel tears come into my eyes and I have to struggle to hide them.

So I say, "Can I borrow your phone, Nana?"

"You want my phone?" and she's grappling for her cordless landline on the little table next to her chair where she keeps all her pills and stuff.

"No, not that one. I mean your mobile phone."

Nana has an old Nokia pay-as-you-go. I hate the thought of taking her stuff but she never uses it, and what can I do? I have to have a phone; it's like being dead without one.

"You'll have to look for it in the drawers," she says, waving her arm over to the sideboard.

I don't really like going through her stuff, but I pull open a drawer and shift a few things around, mainly photos and embroidered bits of lace, old people stuff. Right at the back I dig out the phone.

"Here it is," I say.

Nana puts her new glasses on; the lenses are as thick as the bottom of a beer bottle. I pass her the phone and she turns it over and over in her hand. Old people have to feel things to be sure about them.

I love her so much at this moment I feel my heart could burst. Her fingers are all knobbly and the backs of her hands have blue veins, which stick up under the skin. She's ninety-four, nearly eighty years older than me. All she wants is to reach one hundred and get her telegram from the Queen.

Then she gives me her wonderful, worn out wrinkly smile and says, "There you are lovey, it's still got three pounds on it so you'll be fine and dandy."

She's smiling at me, all pleased with herself that she's got a fortune on her phone to give me. She has no idea what's going on with Dad. But that's good, that's how it's got to be. I've got to go on pretending and Dad will go on pretending until he sorts out this mess. He will sort it, he promised me, didn't he?

She looks so tiny and fragile, like a little knobbly tree, sunk into her chair, a blanket over her knees. She looks even worse than I did in hospital. Can't Dad see how much she needs us? If Nana finds out what he's been up to ... God!

Nana Hat's never done anything wrong in her whole life. "Dad died when I were a baby," she told me once. "Mother brought us up, five kids, all by herself. Always hungry, we was. Mother worked hard all her life and so did I."

Nana Hat didn't steal when she was growing up and they had no money. What would she say if she knew her darling grandson was a thief?

I tap a few keys on the phone and say, "Thank you, Nana, this is great." My voice wobbles a bit but she doesn't seem to notice.

I give her a big hug and kiss and I cling to her for an extra minute. When I straighten she fixes me with her small, brown, glittering eyes. "Mother always knew if we'd done anything. Didn't do no good to hide it from her."

For a second I think she's guessed and she wants me to tell her. I open my mouth to speak and then she starts fussing round my collar and saying, "Make sure you keep warm, don't want you getting ill again."

My heart's beating like a drum. I nearly told her. Oh God.

"Why don't you put the kettle on? We'll have a cuppa before you go off, eh?"

It's a relief to have something to do. When I bring the tea in, Nana's head has drooped and her eyes are closed. For a second I panic and think she's dead.

Then she opens her eyes and perks up, taking her tea with her shaky old hands.

We drink our tea and Nana starts talking about Dad: when he was a little boy and how she had to bring him up after his Mum and Dad died. "It weren't easy and your Dad, he was a bit of a lad," she says.

"What do you mean?"

"Ran around with the wrong crowd. I expect he told you about the boxing club."

I nod.

"It were the courts made him go."

She gives me a look and she can see I hadn't heard about any courts.

"When he were a nipper – only about eleven – he starts pinching things, does your Dad. Course I couldn't give him pocket money."

"What, shoplifting?" Has my Dad been a criminal all his life?

She rearranges the blanket around her knees and then she says, "After that it were the pound coin. He were thirteen when it first come out. He and his friends made moulds and made frozen coins, copies like. They put them in the machines at the arcades. Got found out and came home with a black eye. He was always up to something, your Dad. Wanted to be a millionaire. Used to nag me silly to do the football pools – that's what we had before the Lottery. Silly waste of money. Mother didn't hold with no gambling. 'Got to earn your money in this life,' she always said."

After a bit, she nods off again and I sit there trying to make sense of all this. Dad was into scams and fights when he was a kid. He was up before the courts and they made him take up boxing to get him away from a life of crime. He was always hungry for money, wasn't he? And now look what he's up to.

Nana's eyes open again and she reaches out for her big old red purse. It looks quite thin and empty.

"Here you are darling, call it an early birthday present." She's holding out a ten pound note. "You're nearly sixteen, December seventeeth. You might need some more for that phone."

I take the money and give her a big hug. No one's given me a penny this week.

Then I have a sudden thought and say, "Nana, can I ask where your money comes from? You know, for the flat and your bills and everything?" I know Nana never worked, she was always looking after someone, and she can't have much of a pension.

"Your Dad, of course," murmurs Nana and her eyes close again. "Shut the door on your way out, lovey."

sat nov 15

Saw Scott Fellows today. Doesn't he remember Emily's party last term? He was all over me just before he went to Florida with his parents for the summer. "When I get back babes, you're all mine," he kept whispering in my ear. Then as soon as I get sick he goes off with Paige Butcher.

At least I was with Ryan. Imagine if I'd been on my own. Worse – what if Paige had been there too. But Scott kept giving Ryan funny looks, just cos he's not in our crowd.

But that's what I like about Ryan, he doesn't know anyone, he works in the hospital and he's going off on a road trip to Africa. I can be a completely different person with Ryan if I want. He doesn't know about my family or any of my friends. Not even Sar. Yet.

Maybe I should go with him to Africa, run away, leave this whole mess behind. Nana Hat might even give me some money, although if it all comes from Dad, maybe she'll run out too? Then what will happen to her?

Chapter 7

Saturday night and I'm home alone. Veeve's got a date, Mum's out with the girls and Dad's told her he's got a special business meeting with the partners in the firm. I hope that means he's sorting everything out.

My laptop is on, but Facebook's driving me mad. Everyone pokes me all the time since I was ill. I liked it at first but now I just want to hide. It feels as though everyone can spy on me and see what my Dad's been up to. It's creepy.

Imagine me, Jess Jayne, scared of Facebook. No one would believe it at school. I'm the pretty, popular one, leader of the Jayne family. We were the meanest girl gang in Park Road High before Emily left last summer.

We got together on the first day, me and Sarah and Emily Jane. We decided we'd all put Jayne, with a y, at the end of our names and call ourselves "a family with a twist". Make sure everyone knew who we were right from the start. Even the teachers were nervous when we strolled into class and took up the back row.

But I'm scared all the time now and I can hardly sleep. Every time I close my eyes I see Dad rifling through that wallet in the spare room, and a great fat wad of money in his fingers.

I haven't seen much of Dad this week but he came and sat on my bed last night. His face looked worn out and I couldn't help feeling sorry for him, even though I felt angry at the same time.

"I'm working on it, Jessie," he said. "I'll fix everything, I promise. You're a good girl; we've always looked out for each other, haven't we? Mum and Veeve, they're not tough like us, we know how to stand up for ourselves, like boxers."

I stared up at him. He looked a bit of a mess: his hair needs cutting and it was all limp and greasy. He looked like he'd been wearing the same shirt all week but he's not home much, so Mum probably hasn't noticed. She's too wrapped up in the girls.

"Your Mum hasn't said anything has she?"

I shook my head. "She just thinks I'm in a mood. I told her I don't feel well."

He nodded and dragged a hand across his face.

But then I blurted out, "You won't steal anymore, Dad, will you?"

"No, Jessie, of course I won't. My friends, they'll understand. I'm seeing some people this weekend, going to get it all sorted, I promise, and then your Mum and Veeve don't need to know anything."

There was something about the way he looked at me that made me feel unsure. Was he telling the truth or was it more lies? Like all the lies he's been telling Mum about important meetings around the country.

"Jessie?" he said again, more insistently.

There was nothing I could do; I just had to trust him. So I nodded.

"That's my girl," he said in a more confident voice and then he left.

It took hours to cry myself to sleep.

But now I think of Nana Hat, and how she could have a heart attack and die if she finds out. Then what would I put on Facebook?

When I got sick Sarah told absolutely everybody. She thought it would cheer me up and I did love it. Millions of people asked to be my friend on Facebook. I felt like a celebrity.

I've got 1,356 friends now, five times as many as Veeve. I was aiming for 2,000 by Christmas. But since Dad I don't care anymore.

Emily Jayne Brown anyone heard from jess?
Like • Comment • Share
Hello Kitty nope wots up wiv her
Alix Miller Is she sick again?
Sarah Jayne Lewis her phones not working cant leave a message

I can't put up my status. I don't even want to comment. What would I say? My Dad nicked cash from his friends' wallets?

I keep thinking, Come on Jess, how much could he have taken? A hundred, two hundred, maybe five hundred? It's not the end of the world.

And then I start crying, because it *is* the end of the world.

My Dad's stealing from his friends because he says he hasn't got enough in the bank to pay the bills. And according to Nana Hat he used to do the same when he was a kid. Can't he see what he's doing to all of us, me and Mum and Nana Hat and even my stupid big sister? Doesn't he care?

45

This is pointless so I dry my eyes and pick up my diary. I read back what I wrote about seeing Scott on the beach and about Ryan saying he's going to Africa. Me and Sar do these lists about boys sometimes and see who comes out on top. I decide to do a list and maybe see what Sar thinks.

Ryan or Scott?

Ryan	Scott
my height	almost six foot
thin, freckly skin	big muscles, reddish skin
longish curly hair	short white blond hair
quiet, shy, very sweet	big mouth, big head

Ryan wins. Yaay!

I don't think he's had many girlfriends. Not like Scott, girls all over him all the time, and that slapper, Paige, stealing him from under my nose *when I was sick*!

I've got Ryan's number and now I've got a phone again maybe I'll text him.

Wonder what Sar would think of Ryan?

It's only nine o'clock. What a totally boring Saturday night. Then the house phone rings. I let it ring a few times and then I go downstairs and pick it up. It's Sarah.

"Jess? What's going on with your phone?"

Her voice is so normal my eyes fill up with tears. But Dad's voice hisses in my head, "You can't tell anyone."

I want to ask Sarah to come round, to hang out; to tell her

she wouldn't believe what's happened. She's my best friend, she'd understand. But I can't, I have to keep the secret, keep everyone safe, especially Nana Hat.

So I say to Sarah, "I dropped it in the loo."

"Your iPhone? Your Dad must have gone mad!"

"Mad?" and I imagine Dad frothing at the mouth.

"Hello?" Sarah says.

"Hello ... sorry ... no, no he's fine," I stutter back. "You know what he's like."

Then Sarah says, "He'll get you another one."

That's what her parents would do, isn't it? They're minted, like my parents. Well, like mine *were*. Only now it's all changed. He definitely wouldn't get me another iPhone now if I broke mine.

"I'm so bored," says Sarah. "Can't you come over?"

"No!" I say quickly, and then I give a silly giggle. "I'm shattered, Sar. I was asleep when you rang." I can't face seeing her with all these secrets in my head.

"Oh, soz babes. OK, see you then, sleep tight."

Her phone clicks off and I'm all alone again.

I go back up to my room and flick back through my diary. I kept it all through the illness. The doctors hardly told me anything so I tried to write down all the things they thought were wrong with me, like hepatitis and something called lupus, which I'd never even heard of.

Then, after doing all their horrible tests, they said to Mum, "We can't rule out a malignancy, Mrs Fitzgerald."

Malignancy turned out to be a polite medical term for the C word.

Cancer. The word which is more unmentionable than sex or even rude words. All through September and October I got worse and worse. I couldn't eat, couldn't go to school. No one really knew what was wrong with me.

Then they said, "We think you have a lymphoma, Jess, but we're not sure, yet."

I didn't understand what they were saying and then I found out.

Facebook is still open on my laptop. I scroll to September, even though I've read it a million times.

Jess Jayne I've got the big C. Cancer

And then I read all the comments and it makes me feel even lonelier because I can't talk to anyone.

I open my diary again and flick back to September. It's like picking at a scab.

sep 14
Monica Jones in the bed opposite died yesterday. She was forty-three with two kids, so she was old. But not as old as Nana Hat. They think I have cancer too. There's no point in pretending and saying malignancy. It's cancer. I know it. They're doing one more test before they start chemo on Friday. Then my hair will fall out.

I'm not even sixteen yet

Every time I read that page I feel the same fear in the pit of my stomach. I came so close. I even planned my funeral: the playlist, the food. I thought I was going to die.

They never said I could die, of course, they pretended the chemo would zap all the bad cells. But look at Monica Jones – bright and bubbly, chatting to her kids one minute and then a week later, dead.

"That's what cancer can do to you," Doris in the next bed had said. She didn't even put her teeth in anymore.

But I didn't have cancer. That one final test did it.

sep 15

It's not CANCER! I don't have cancer. I don't have cancer. I DON'T HAVE CANCER!!

I'm not going to die like Monica Jones. I've got sarcoid, which makes you very, very ill but it doesn't kill you. The doctors said I'll get better slowly – Completely Utterly Totally BETTER.

In one short minute the whole world turned back the other way round.

"It will take time," said the doctor, "you've been very ill. You'll have to have more tests and scans to be sure we haven't missed anything."

"But I'm not going to die?"

He looked really pleased, "No, you're going to live for a very long time, I hope."

"As long as Nana Hat," said Veeve, and I looked round at

Mum and Dad and Veeve and everyone was laughing and smiling and looking so relieved.

I yelled out right across the ward, "Nana Hat wants to be 100 and so do I!"

I was going to live and live and live.

Everyone went wild. I came home from hospital and it was like I'd won the X Factor. We had this big party, all my friends, Veeve's mates from the Sixth Form, the girls from the Marina and Dad's business friends. I lay on the sofa, the absolute centre of attention.

"You've been saved from the jaws of death," said Nana Hat, and she pushed over on her Zimmer frame and gave me a big kiss and a twenty pound note.

Everyone went mad on Facebook too.

Jess Jayne It's not cancer, it's sarcoid!!!! dead weird, BUT IT DOESN'T KILL YOU ☺
Like • Comment • Share
Karl Reece I've googled it ... you don't need chemo. YAAAY!!
Hello Kitty The one and only Jess Jayne maaaan you are soo speshul
Emily Jayne Brown my mum lit a candle for you in church today
Alix Miller Mazing! Samir says brill 2. I'll tell Kim and Steven and EVERYONE!!
Sarah Jayne Lewis we're gonna party forever babee ☺☺☺

I didn't know that my life was going to fall through the floor for a second time before my sixteenth birthday.

Chapter 8

Ryan

I'm under the van on Sunday morning when my phone beeps. I pull myself up. It's a text from Jess.

meet up oyster beds 2 ☺

Her phone must be back on and she's asking to see me. Wow! I text back.

gr8 l8r

Hope she thinks that's cool enough.

It's a funny place to meet; there's nothing there, not even a shop, but I need to take the van out anyway, test the new brake system. She'll be impressed if I drive there, won't she? I'll spray air freshener before I leave.

I love being under my van, the smell of grease and the weight of a spanner in my hand. Dad's a mechanic, taught me everything. I could hand him any tool by the time I was ten. He knows all about spares and the best scrap yards.

Dad loves the yards. We spend hours on a Saturday picking over old wrecks for parts. The garage is full of stuff. Got my alloy wheels and a brand new door from the yard, and we're going next week to look for lights. Dad reckons we could also get a radio/stereo if we slip the guy a couple of quid.

"You'll need everything you can get to drive through Africa," says Dad, and it gives me such a nervy feeling in my stomach. Sometimes I even think of asking him to come with me. I mean I'm looking forward to it, in some ways – fixing the van, keeping it running – but I don't know if I really want to go on my own.

"Stinks in here." It's James. He's drinking a can of *my* Red Bull.

"Oi, give me that," I make a grab for the can but he dodges out the way. "You know Mum says you're too young."

"*Mum says, mum says,*" he copies in a silly voice. He's such a cocky little jerk.

He was quite a sweet little kid when he was in junior school, but he's changed in the past few months since he turned fourteen. He's bulked up. And he's good at sports, not like me. He's a striker in the first eleven football team. He's got Mum's straight black hair and green eyes. The girls go mad over him. Makes me feel like such a loser.

I especially hate it when he brings his girlfriends round for dinner, showing them off like football trophies. Francine or Trace, or the latest one, Pippa. Always pretty.

"That heap of junk won't get on the ferry," he says, chucking the empty can in the back of the van.

"It'll get all the way through the Sahara...."

James gives a loud snort. "The Sahara's bigger than America, you'll get so lost. They have sand vipers, pythons, rattlesnakes, cobras....", he's ticking them off on his fingers, "... then there's the flies, scorpions. People die of thirst just looking at the Sahara. It gets up to 50°C and they don't have ice-cream vans."

James is way cleverer than me. He's in all the top sets and he's a year ahead in Maths. Mum wants him to go to uni.

Dad thinks that's why I want to go to Africa. "Don't have to prove nothing to us, Ryan," he says. "You and James are different, that's all. James could do with some of your kindness."

But who cares when you're a genius? I didn't even finish school. I have to do something with my life before it all pours away like sand in the desert.

Max wants to climb Everest – it's the only "abroad" he'll consider. He's been emailing famous climbers and trying to get on an expedition. Now that's a proper ambition. Not like selling jeans outside a Nairobi uni to desperate students who'd rather be in London scrubbing floors. But Africa, well, it's a goal, something to aim for. And learning how to fix the van at least means I'm doing something useful.

I've always loved cars. My bedroom is covered with pictures of cars, bikes, vans and even trucks, torn out of magazines. I love driving too. I've taken the van out on a few short trips. I'm going to ask Jess if she wants to go with me next weekend to Brighton for the day. She's not like other girls, Jessica Fitzgerald.

After that bloke Scott went off and we were left hanging about on the beach, I thought she wasn't interested anymore. But then she said, "Walk a bit?"

I gave a nod and we went off down the beach.

"I don't remember you at Park Road," she said.

"I went to school on the Island. I got some GCSEs but I

didn't go on to Sixth Form College and A-Levels," I said. No point in pretending I'm a boffin, is there?

"I'm thinking of leaving school," she said. "I'm thinking of leaving home....", and suddenly she was talking about how she hates her life and she has to do something to change it and she doesn't think she can wait much longer.

"You must think I'm mental." Her face was hidden by her hair, which had been blown about by the wind. It was almost four in the afternoon, and the sky would be pitch dark in a few minutes.

"I understand," I said. I wanted to tell Jessica Fitzgerald how I'd screwed up school and James was the boffin in our family, off to uni like a prince. And me, Ryan O'Neill? I was heading for the scrap yard where I picked up my windscreen wipers and my scratched, but perfectly serviceable, bumper. Max's voice came into my ear, "Steady mate, only the first date," so I just said, "Well, yeah, know what you mean. That's why I'm going to Africa."

She hadn't said anything but she'd sort of looked at me a bit like the way she'd looked at that Scott bloke.

I could hear the sea pulling up and down over the beach and the air smelt of salt and chips wafting over from the street and I could have stood there with Jessica Fitzgerald staring at me as if I was somebody special forever.

I'm pulled back to the garage by the sound of a car in the road. James has turned up with Pippa. Her Dad dropped her off in his Merc. She wrinkles up her nose when she sees the van.

"Eugh," she says, as she and James go off, hooting with laughter.

I do a bit more work and then I go and get cleaned up to meet Jess. When I've finished another text comes in: **call me, lee**. I have to think for a minute and then I remember. I catch sight of myself in the bathroom mirror – my cheeks have gone a bit red.

It's Leanne, the girl from the end-of-summer party; September sometime, wasn't it? Max and me were sort of on a bender, I can't even remember how it started but we ended up on pints of beer with vodka shots. There were two girls. Mine was Leanne; she was over from Portsmouth, staying with her cousin, Denny, on the Island. Me and Denny used to hang out in school and it was his beach party.

Leanne and I were dancing. I don't usually dance so it must have been the drink, and then we went off to the beach huts. One of them was open and she took my hand and led me inside.

It was all because of James. He never stops going on about me being gay. Only he never says it in front of Mum and Dad. Golden boy, isn't he? With his exams and his girlfriends.

The night before the party, he came into my room, picking all my stuff up, having a go.

"Bet you never done it," he says in his mocking voice.

He's got this look on his face like he has.

He's only fourteen. How could he have? It's illegal isn't it? I didn't even know about sex at his age, not really. Max told me on my fifteenth birthday in the park. He opened my first can of beer for me and told me all about girls and sex and how to pull.

So at the beach party, Lee and I were so drunk and all I could think was, I'll show that cocky jerk of a little brother.

But after the party she must have gone back to Portsmouth. I didn't see her again. I didn't care, I wasn't in love. I didn't even tell Max.

She had soft skin, very pale, like vanilla ice cream. She was all right, I suppose. I don't really want to see her again, but it seems rude not to call if she's asked me to. I feel a bit nervous as I get her number up.

She answers straight away. "Where are you?"

"At home," I say. Bit of a strange question.

"Me too."

"OK," I say.

"I'm pregnant and it's yours...."

The phone feels like it's burning a hole in my ear.

"It's yours, Ryan, you and me in the beach hut. Remember?"

I'm staring at the van, wrench in my hand, and it's the only thing that feels real.

"We need to meet," she says. "Ryan? You listening? I haven't told anyone. I only found out this morning. What are we going to do?"

Do? I don't know, do I?

I think of all the people who will find out: Mum, Dad ... James, oh God, his smug little face.

And what will Max say? "Mate, what you gone and done now?"

I count on my fingers: September, October, now it's November, how many months is that?

"Ryan? Answer me, say something, I'm terrified. My Dad's going to kill me. Ryan?"

"OK!" I yell back. My voice breaks with the strain and I croak. "Give me a chance. What do you expect me to say? I don't have the handbook on this. Christ, just give me a sec."

I want to run, fire up the van and drive straight to Africa. That's all I can think about. I want to drive there now. Not stop for supplies, nothing, just go, go, go.

Chapter 9
Jess

"Where's Dad?"

It's nearly one and I'm having a piece of toast. Veeve's still in bed and Mum's ironing a blouse. She's meeting the girls at the Clubhouse for coffee.

"He's out all day on business," she says, spraying water on the blouse.

"On a Sunday?" Isn't she a bit suspicious yet?

She gives me a cold look and says, "Have you two been arguing again?"

"No."

"Hmm," she says and tweaks the blouse. "He's been in a funny mood this week. I know he told you the business is having problems, but you don't need to have a go at him. Veeve doesn't."

That is so unfair. But then I wonder what he has really told her.

"Did he tell you what sort of problems?" I ask casually.

"Oh, you know, cash flow, because of the banks all over the world, the credit crunch," she says, sounding vague.

Mum's like Veeve, they don't understand business. Not like me and Dad.

"But everyone's in the same boat," she goes on, "as your Dad says. He's sorting it out with Anthony Perrins." She unplugs the iron and looks around for the hanger.

"Aren't you worried, Mum?" I say in a small voice.

"Well of course I'm worried, Jess. These are worrying times," she says, a bit too quickly. "But you know your Dad; he pulled himself up by his bootstraps from nothing. He's not going to let a bit of a problem with the banks get in his way."

But as she fusses around with her blouse I can see she's all stiff and tense.

Then her phone goes, "Angela? Five minutes and I'll be with you."

She picks up the hanger and sweeps out of the room, calling over her shoulder, "Cold chicken in the fridge for lunch, make sure you eat something."

How much longer before Mum and Veeve find out? I really don't want to be around when they do.

I catch the bus to go and meet Ryan and sit upstairs. As we get near the top end of the Island the tide is in and the sea is spreading out either side of Langstone Bridge. Ryan doesn't seem to know the oyster beds very well. It'll be fun to show him. Hardly anyone comes around in winter, so he'll like it there.

Ryan's quiet, not like Scott and the other boys from school. Ryan would never fit in with them – always smoking, mucking about drunk or stoned, bragging about who's doing it. I used to be in the centre: pretty, popular, never single. Last summer Scott only had eyes for me. I wouldn't have given Ryan a second look. But now ... well now everything's changed and I'm just glad that someone, anyone, wants me.

I didn't eat the chicken and now I'm hungry. I finger the ten pound note in my pocket which Nana gave me yesterday. I'd better make it last, I can get some crisps from the garage before I meet Ryan.

Sarah used to bring me a six pack of salt and vinegar in hospital.

"Mum says the salt will help with the sickness," she told me.

I'm addicted now. I wrote it on Facebook and then everyone kept bringing me crisps, it was great.

Jess Jayne Fitzgerald 12 packs of crisps and i still lost weight today
Like • Comment • Share
Hello Kitty u must be minus size zero now
Karl Reece I ate 22 packs in one go when i was ten
Sarah Jayne Lewis yaay shopping babes new ski jacket ☺
Alix Miller did you get the maths homework?
Hello Kitty stuff maths maaan go shopping ☺

When I get off the bus I head for the garage shop. But then I spot Dad. What's he doing here? He can't be having a business meeting, there's nowhere to meet anyone.

He's over by the cash machine on the wall. I look about for his car but I can't see it. He's fiddling about with his credit card, but as I watch it gets rejected twice. He told me his cards were all maxed out, so what's going on?

I start to get this creepy-crawly feeling over my skin, like before when he scared me in the bathroom last week. He hasn't spotted me but he's looking around as if he's checking that no one sees his pin number. He looks like a nervous bird watching out for cats.

But maybe he's getting things sorted, I start to tell myself. Maybe Anthony Perrins is bailing him out, maybe Dad just panicked and we're going to be all right.

I've almost convinced myself he's getting money out to pay back everything he stole last Sunday from the lunch visitors when the card pops out. He grabs it and turns it over in his fingers. He looks furious. Something's not right here. He starts to twist his neck around to see if anyone is there and then he sees me and his face goes white.

I go over but I don't know what to say.

His voice shakes a bit as he says, "What are you doing here?"

"Getting crisps," I say. "Feeling a bit sick."

He nods and I wait, thinking that any minute now he'll tell me it's OK, everything's sorted and that I don't need to worry anymore.

Then I look down at his hand and he's trying to flip over the credit card. Something makes me reach out and grab it.

I can't believe my eyes. I stare at the name on the card. I must be wrong. I must be.

It says Anthony Perrins. Dad's partner.

"Where did you get this?"

"Give me that." Dad snatches the card and gives me a shove.

I lose my balance and topple into the wall, hitting the side of my face. It hurts so much I let out a yelp and Dad lifts his hand. But his fingers close into a fist and suddenly I'm really scared. I step backwards and stumble as my ankle turns and I crumple in a heap on the hard concrete.

Dad just stands there, glaring down at me as if it's all my fault.

My face hurts and I put my hand up to feel the damage. I'm not bleeding, but I can feel a bump beginning to swell over my cheekbone and the skin is all grazed and broken. Dad doesn't put out a hand to help me up, or say he's sorry, or ask me if I'm all right. What's the matter with him?

An old green Rover pulls up and a man jumps out, slams the door behind him and strides past us to the shop. He gives us a look but he doesn't say anything. He's probably thinking it's a domestic. I almost wish he would do something – yell at Dad or take a swing at him. I even look over my shoulder to see if Ryan is coming, but there's nobody.

Dad leans over me and hisses, "Look, stay out of it, Jess, OK?" Then he turns and walks off towards the bridge.

"What would Nana Hat say?" I call out through my tears, but he doesn't even look back.

The man comes out, gets into his Rover and drives off. He doesn't even look at me.

I can't believe what just happened. Dad's hurt me for the very first time in my life, and he doesn't care. He's committing fraud now, and what's going to happen when the police catch him and it all comes out in court? I suddenly think of the Gina Butcher scandal. Was Dad guilty after all? Is it going to be like that all over again?

The Gina Butcher scandal is the reason me and Veeve

didn't go to Eversleigh, the private school. Instead we had to go to Park Road High. "Full of all those hooligans from the estate," Mum had yelled at Dad. I was so scared, that's why I grabbed Emily and Sarah on the first day and made them set up the Jayne family with me. A posh-girl gang to keep the estate kids away from us. The funny thing is, Park Road's OK really, and there's plenty of boys. Eversleigh is all girls.

In the end it was proven that Dad hadn't done anything. Gina Butcher was in admin in Dad's firm before he was made a partner. Money went missing and she went to the papers and told some story, accusing Dad of stealing the money. Dad said he and Gina had never really got on. "Nasty mouth she has," he told us, "always had it in for me for some reason."

Mum called the Sunday paper a rag. "All it prints is gossip," she used to say in a loud voice, especially in front of Angela and the girls. "It's a load of rubbish; no one takes any notice of it."

We all went round saying, "Gina Butcher, load of rubbish," for years. But of course, people did take notice and I suppose things were very difficult for Dad and Mum for a while.

I was only nine, I didn't really understand. Dad was cleared but Eversleigh didn't like the publicity. They said something about being the wrong sort of school for us, and said they thought we would be better off at Park Road.

Gina's daughter is Paige Butcher. We hate each other. Even more so now she's with Scott.

Stuffed

So did Dad steal from his firm all those years ago? Money was much tighter when I was little, all the presents and the foreign holidays only started when I was about nine. Didn't last long, did it? When Antony Perrins finds out about his credit card he's bound to think about the Gina Butcher scandal.

My cheek is really painful; I bruise easily since the illness. Dad knows that, Dad should have ... He didn't even look normal. Maybe he's gone mad.

I hear a horn honking. A battered old camper van with yellow doors and a bumper that looks as though it's falling off pulls into the forecourt. It's Ryan. I quickly wipe a sleeve over my tears and hope he doesn't notice my red eyes and swollen cheek.

"Hey," he calls out, jumping down from the van. He's fiddling about with the door handle when I go over. I've got a tissue out and I've covered my cheek with it, but he's going to see it sooner or later. I'll have to come up with some excuse. How could I tell the truth? What would that sound like?

"Hey," I say.

He gives the door handle another twist and says, "It's a bit battered, my old van, but it gets around. Hop in." Then he zips round the front of the van.

When I climb in Ryan can only see my right cheek. He's messing about with the dashboard and the gear lever, a bit of a frown on his face. I know he's doing the van up, so maybe there's a technical problem. I'd rather he concentrated on

65

the van than on me and my face, anyway.

The van jerks into life and we take off down the road. There's a couple of sharp bends coming up and Ryan's focused on his driving so I don't distract him.

"Do I turn after the sign?" he says, and I nod.

It's very tight here and we are bumping over the potholes on the unmade track that runs parallel to the beach. Then the track opens onto the rough pebbly ground above the oyster beds. We could have a lot of fun driving around this bit, but Ryan pulls over and turns the engine off. We sit there in silence, but not a nice, comfy silence. He hasn't noticed my face yet; in fact, he's hardly looked at me. I know he's shy, not big-headed like Scott, but it's almost as though he doesn't want to see me. Weird.

What's changed since our texts this morning? Maybe he's had second thoughts about going out with me. Who wants a girlfriend who's been so sick she's almost disappearing? Scott lost interest as soon as I fell ill. I stood on the scales this morning. I've lost another kilo.

I'm just about to suggest a walk when there's a cheery knock on the window. Some tall thin guy on a bike, with a woollen hat pulled halfway down his forehead, is grinning and staring in at us.

Ryan jerks into life. "Max, mate," he yells and practically throws himself out of the van.

He knows how to make a girl feel wanted, does Ryan.

Not.

Chapter 10

Ryan

I've never been so pleased to see anyone in my life. I can feel Jess staring at me from inside the van as I wrench open the door and almost jump on Max.

"Mate, steady on." Max is laughing and pushing me off. "I thought that was your heap of rust going past me on the road. What's up?"

"Nothing," I say. He sees Jess in the van and gives me a grin. "Just hanging out," I add.

I try to catch his eye but he's leaning forward to get a better look.

"You gonna introduce us?" he says.

I'm trying to block his eye line into the van, hoping by some miracle he'll suddenly be able to read my mind and find out all about Lee. Max will know what to do, but I can hardly tell him now.

Then I hear the sound of the passenger door opening, it creaks really badly. Jess comes round the side of the van to where we're standing and she's got a tissue over her cheek.

So I say, "Jess, Max. Max, Jess."

Jess stands there with her head lowered, nursing her cheek. Part of me wishes she'd just disappear, but another part can't help noticing how great she's looking. She's added some red to her hair and she's wearing purple as usual. I want to kiss her and I want to tell her to walk away. I'm so confused.

Max says, "You got something in your eye?"

Jess shakes her head and lowers her hand. There's a swollen red lump on her cheek. Is that her illness?

"Need an ice-pack on that," says Max. He knows about first aid from climbing.

"Sorry?" says Jess.

We're back to that again, and I'm the one who should be saying sorry. Sorry I asked you out and wanted to be your boyfriend. Sorry I'm being off with you today, and sorry I'm too scared to tell you why. Sorry I got another girl pregnant.

Max is rummaging about in the backpack he always carries and he's got a little silver packet out. He tears it open and hands Jess a wipe. I get a whiff of antiseptic.

"This might help," he says in his cheery voice.

She mutters, "Thanks," and cleans her face a bit but she's wincing with the pain.

"Here, let me," says Max, and I'm standing around like a spare part again while my best friend administers healing and comfort to my potential girlfriend. But she won't want to know me when she finds out about Lee.

"Better?" says Max and Jess nods, her hair covering her face again.

"How did you do it?" he asks, glancing at me.

"Tripped," says Jess, and she's raising her head to look at me.

I feel lower than an ant. I didn't ask her, did I? She'll think I don't care, when I do. I really do, but now there's Lee and a baby. I should just get in the van and drive off. Give

Jessica Fitzgerald a lucky escape.

I stuff my hands in the pockets of my jeans and look away. I don't want her to see what I think are maybe tears starting up.

Jess takes a couple of steps and her legs wobble on the uneven ground.

Max puts out his hand and says, "You'd better hang on to me, make sure you stay on your feet."

Jess shoots him a really grateful sort of look and before I can do anything she takes his hand. My best mate and my girlfriend are holding hands and I'm standing watching them like its OK. I can hear James in my ear, "Loser."

"I ride over here sometimes," says Max in this really chatty voice, and he's looking at me and raising his eyebrows, trying to get me to join in. But all I can see is his hand gripping Jess's thin little fingers. Max has got quite a grip, needs it for the climbing. I'm worried he's going to crush her bones or something. "My Dad used to bring me when he wanted to try out a new tent or a stove," Max is rattling on. "Remember when we had sausages in the rain, mate?" He's staring at me and flicking his eyes down to Jess's hand. He wants me to take over. I feel as if I've turned into a statue.

"Outdoorsy, is he?" says Jess in this really small voice.

"Yeah," says Max. "He owns the camping shop on the High Street."

I glower at Max and he finally stops talking.

There's an awkward silence until I say, "We're just hanging out, wanna come?" and I nod towards the oyster beds stretching out into the water.

Max raises Jess's hand in my direction. "No, I've gotta go," he says, and then grinning at Jess he goes on in a cowboy drawl, "but I'll leave you in the real good hands of my pardner here."

Jess smiles and Max passes her hand to mine and she shyly takes it. How can this be so hard? But I hold her hand, because it seems like the easiest option.

"I'll be off then, see you in the Dog and Deer later," and with a cheery wave, Max gets back on his bike and pedals off. I watch him disappear. Now what?

We wander off, not speaking, and turn onto one of the spits of land which goes out to sea. We walk all the way to the end, where the ground falls away into chalk beds.

I'm kicking through the chalk, almost without thinking, looking for flints. I like looking for flints. They were the first proper tools. I watched someone make a flint knife on TV once – he sheared an entire fleece off a sheep with it. "Sharp as a surgeon's knife," he'd said.

The water's lapping at our feet and the chalk goes right out to sea. It sparkles under the water, which is transparent, like there are no secrets here.

But I've got a guilty secret and when I tell Jess she won't want to go out with me anymore.

"I come here all the time," says Jess.

I wonder who she comes here with? There's a burnt-out log on some blackened stones on the beach. People must come down here to party. I bet that Scott bloke brings girls here at night for bonfires, and to make out. Maybe that's what Jess wanted.

Without realising it, I've let go of Jess's hand and she's fallen behind me. I walk further over the chalk. I'm standing there all on my own and I just want to howl and howl at the sea. Lee wants to meet up. I'll have to drive to Portsmouth. What about me and Jess?

Me and Jess. What a joke.

Jess has come up behind me and she's got her iPod out with the wire hanging in her hand.

I turn and stare at her like we just met.

"Have you heard this track?" she asks. She hands me one earphone and puts the other one in her ear.

It seems such a normal, everyday question, when life has suddenly hurtled into what feels like the paranormal.

I have to move closer so we can share the earphones. I can smell her scent. It makes me think of peaches. Her hair is blowing around and it flicks against my cheek and gets tangled up in the wire. I reach out and start to untangle it, and there's a look in her eyes that is sort of like sadness and gladness all mixed up together. That's how I feel too. I'm glad we made it this far, but I feel so sad and scared too, and I'm sure she can see it in my eyes. Maybe she just thinks I'm nervous about getting close. Well, I am, aren't I? I'd be nervous anyway, but now, with Lee and a baby....

"What do you think?" she says.

I realise that I wasn't really listening to the music, but now I try to concentrate. There's this bloke with a flat, London-type accent, chanting out lyrics, and there's quite a cool band playing behind him. The song is about reasons to be cheerful.

I raise a questioning eyebrow at Jess.

She grins and says, "It's Ian Dury and the Blockheads. They were a punk band in the seventies. My blood guy got me into it in hospital."

"Blood guy?"

"Phlebotomist. They're the ones who take blood from you to test it."

Her hair blows in her face again and she reaches up and twists it round her fingers. My hair doesn't move much in the wind, but I wish Jess would put her fingers in it right now.

"I hate blood," I say.

"Me too. But there was one phlebotomist who was always kind to me. I called him Bloodguy. His hair was short and spiky and it was grey at the sides, like my Dad's. He wore a pink rubber bracelet – I think he was gay."

That word again, like a horrible reminder of the mess I'm in and how I got into it in the first place; James mocking me, "you're gay", "you haven't even done it have you?" etc, etc.

Why did I have to prove anything to that little jerk?

But Jess is still talking, "They took blood every single day when I was in hospital."

To be honest I don't know much about what it's really like for the patients. I just run the appointments.

"I was crying once because another vein had burst. It happened all the time and they usually didn't care. Just kept poking you until they got a new vein. In your ankle, your leg, anywhere."

"I thought they could only take blood from your arm."

She shakes her head, "That's what everyone thinks. Veeve, my big sister, cried once when she saw my bruises."

My eyes flick to her cheek and she lowers her head. They wouldn't take it from there, would they?

"Bloodguy saw me crying," says Jess, "and he took over, sent the other bloke to the next bed. He gave me his earphones and said, 'Listen to this.' It was Ian Dury and the Blockheads, singing about all these reasons to be cheerful. I hardly noticed him sticking the needle in the back of my hand, even though he had to do it twice to get the vein properly. Now I love that song."

We listen to another track and then she says, "Ian Dury had polio and couldn't walk properly. He died of cancer when he was 58."

"But you won't die of cancer...." I stop, scared she might realise I peeked at her notes.

"Nope," she says. "I didn't have cancer. Lucky me."

She doesn't look as though she feels that lucky. She just looks sort of numb.

We stand like that, listening to the band – the Blockheads, I like that – and our shoulders are touching, which feels so good. But I can't put my arm round her, can I? It wouldn't be right after Lee's phone call.

When the track ends, Jess turns off the iPod and the gulls take over, screaming off the end of the spit like they're laughing at me, like James does.

"My brother's a blockhead," I say. I've never said that word before and it feels just right for him.

She doesn't ask why, she just winds her earphones round and round her iPod, slips it back in her jacket pocket, looks up at me with her numb eyes and says, "My Dad's a blockhead."

And I kiss her, right there, right on the mouth and her lips are so soft I almost can't feel them at first.

Something or someone has hurt Jessica Fitzgerald and it's not just being ill that's done it.

I don't want to be the next one to hurt her. I feel like I'm falling in love with her.

I didn't feel like this in the beach hut with Lee.

Chapter 11
Jess

"Why haven't you got your uniform on?" Mum says. Veeve is staring at me over the breakfast table and I glance at Mum. Mum doesn't look up from her phone. She's texting Angela. But she says, "Have you got an appointment?"

Veeve frowns and I give her a smug look. "You know I'm at hospital today, Mum. Have you forgotten?"

Mum looks up from the screen and she's almost sympathetic. "Bloods?"

I nod, "Plus hours and hours waiting in Imaging, today *and* tomorrow. Then I've got the Consultant on Wednesday. I can't go into school, can I?"

"What about your work?" Mum's already gone back to texting.

"Sarah will keep me up to date; you know she never misses a day."

Veeve snorts but Mum nods and says, "Try and get in before the end of the week."

She glances up as Dad comes into the kitchen. I didn't know he was here; he wasn't home when I got back from seeing Ryan yesterday. I give him a hopeful look but he doesn't meet my eyes. Has he sorted things out?

He's still in his pyjamas. I can't remember ever seeing him in pyjamas at eight o'clock in the morning. Why doesn't Mum say something?

"Haven't you got work today, Dad?" Veeve asks, finally useful for something.

"Slow day at the office," says Dad with a cheery grin.

Mum doesn't seem bothered and she says, "Ronny, give Jess a twenty, she won't be in school until Thursday and Veeve needs extra this week, art project or something ... ooh, Angela," she finishes with a squeal as a text comes in.

I butter a piece of toast and hand it to Dad. He's sitting in his usual seat and he's picked up the salt pot for his egg. He puts it down again and takes the toast. Our eyes lock. For the first time he notices my cheek. He doesn't even flinch, just looks back down at his plate and slices the top off his boiled egg.

I can't believe it.

Mum went mad last night when she saw my face. "Who did that to you?" she screamed.

She caught me unawares; I nearly burst into tears and told her about Dad. But he wasn't there anyway, and Ryan had been so strange and distant at the oyster beds after he kissed me, all I wanted to do was crawl into bed and write in my diary.

So I swallowed really hard and muttered, "I was walking on a pebbly bit of beach and fell over. I felt a bit faint, I think."

She went all Florence Mum then, and fussed about. She made me go straight to bed and brought me up tea and toast; she even sat on the end of the bed for a minute, which she absolutely never does. The house was very quiet. Veeve was out and Dad had disappeared and I decided that this was the right moment.

"Mum, you know you said Dad's business was going...."

Then the house phone started to ring and she was gone.

"Ronny?" Mum says now as Dad reaches for the salt. Dad ignores her but I can see she's got her impatient look on her face. "Money for the girls?"

Get out of this one, I think, but I feel like bursting into tears. I don't want Dad to be found out, I want things to go back to the way they were, with Dad being funny and spoiling me, Mum going out with the girls and me getting better and organising the party with Sar.

"Haven't been to the cash machine, take it out of the drawer for today and I'll get some money later," says Dad.

I can't believe how cool his voice is as he lies to Mum.

She gives him a confused look and then says slowly, "OK, but there's not much left in there either."

Dad doesn't say anything and I watch as she goes to a little drawer inside the top cupboard where she keeps emergency cash and pulls out two notes. She hands us both a fiver.

"But Mum...." whines Veeve.

Mum cuts her off, "Stop moaning Veeve. Honestly, sometimes I can't believe you're the eldest." Veeve looks so crushed I throw her a sympathetic look. This isn't her fault, or Mum's, or mine.

Now I have to keep myself out of the house most of the days this week and I have no idea what to do.

tues nov 18

I'm out of school and I'm already bored. Not even enough hospital appointments. Never thought I'd say that, but at least they kept me busy.

I can't show my face in school while it's still so swollen, but Sar wants to meet up later at lunch time.

And no money!! I've almost spent the ten pounds Nana gave me, but I can't touch my savings. That's supposed to be for college. I checked my bank account online. I've got loads, all my birthday and Xmas money and the extra Dad gives me and Veeve, which he calls our 'bonuses'. But I won't take it out. Not yet anyway.

Dad goes out all day, but not to work. I think he just goes and sits in the park. How much longer can he keep this up? I'm honestly beginning to wonder if all this is my fault because he spent so much money on me when I was ill.

All I want is this nightmare to END.

I wrote exactly the same sentence in my diary the day before I got my diagnosis, when Monica Jones in the bed opposite died.

I want this nightmare to END.

Why have I ended up feeling like this TWICE????!!!!

Dad's messing up our lives and when Mum and Veeve find out it'll get worse, not better. They'll blame me for not telling them.

So I'm stuffed whatever I do.

"OK, spill and don't spare me the details."

Lunchtime I'm in Starbucks on the High Street with Sarah and for a second I worry that she knows everything because her Dad is the manager of the local bank where my Dad has all his accounts.

Then I realise she means Ryan. I told her a bit about it the other day. I know Ryan was a bit weird on Sunday but he kissed me and it was so sweet and gentle. After Dad pushed me over and that horrible swollen cheek, it was Ryan who took away all the pain. It doesn't matter that he's not part of Scott's group, neither am I anymore. So I say, "He's a great kisser," and Sarah's face lights up.

"Excellent! What's his star sign and what about his shoes. Trainers, loafers or boots?"

I laugh and laugh, I think I'm never going to stop.

"What?" says Sarah, grinning at me. "You need to know for proper compatibility. Me and Helmut split up over his shoes."

"Helmut was *not* your boyfriend!" I splutter. I don't ever want to stop laughing, it feels so good. I haven't laughed for weeks.

"So?" she says and takes a slurp of her smoothie.

She's ordered the most fattening drinks and cakes in the cafe. Her mum has said I need to put on weight so Sarah's made it a mission. She's always got a new mission on the go.

Like when she got our whole class to get the same ringtone; to have a 'corporate identity', she said. We nearly drove the teachers mad when we all played it at the same time. It sounded amazing.

Sarah's phone goes and she's busy for a few minutes chatting. I've managed to convince her that I've had a reaction to a new drug for my illness and that's why I haven't been in school this week.

She wasn't too bothered. Sarah doesn't skip school, her parents are much stricter than my parents, but she's really only interested in the social life. She's single at the moment and she hasn't got her eye on anyone. "They're all so immature," she says. "You're so lucky with a working man. I'm sick of schoolboys."

She's right. Being with Ryan is taking me away from my stuffed up life. Maybe he'll even take me all the way to Africa; I could use my savings.

"Describe him in minute detail." Sarah's looking at me expectantly.

I grin and say, "A bit taller than me, five eight maybe, thin, well not too thin, and he doesn't wear his jeans round his bum."

Sarah gives an approving nod; only the dumb boys in school show off most of their boxers.

"He's got pale skin; I don't think he'll tan well, but no spots!" We laugh. "And his hair is so gorgeous, totally curly and he grows it so he's even got ringlets down the side of his face and at the back. It's darkish brown and he's got thin brown eyebrows. I think he shaved through the right one once because you can still see a bit of a line there. No piercings...."

"Hate weird piercings," Sarah says.

We both pull a face.

"Tongue bars," I say.

"Privates!" she shrieks, and we scream-laugh.

"Yeah, but he would look cute with a bar through his

eyebrow. He's probably not allowed because of his job in the hospital," I say.

Sar nods, "Ryan sounds hot."

I look at her and I'm so enjoying sharing all this with my best friend again. But there's so much I'm not telling her.

"Mmm, hot? Not sure about that. But he's very, very sweet."

"Sweet's good."

"He's got a camper van he's doing up. It smells a bit."

"Yuck."

"Yeah, but he's very proud of it. He's going to take it on this big road trip."

I stop. Don't say where, I tell myself. Sar won't understand.

"I might go with him."

"Cool. Take next summer off; school's out early after exams. You could go for at least six weeks."

I stare at her for a minute. She doesn't get it, does she? But how can she? I haven't told her my life has fallen apart. No one knows except me and my Dad, who has stolen money, maybe even from *her* Dad's bank. And how Nana Hat might have a heart attack and die if she finds out. And to my horror, tears start up in my eyes and I'm scrabbling in my pocket for a tissue.

"Jess, babes, what is it? I knew something was up. You've been so *weird* lately. What is it?"

And they're there, in my mouth, the words. I need to tell her everything, and I would have but suddenly a voice says, "Looks like you need another clean tissue."

It's Max. I'm almost as pleased to see him as Ryan was on

Sunday. Max has appeared like a cowboy riding in on his horse to save the day.

I can't speak for a minute, I just take the tissue and dry my eyes. I can feel Sarah waiting impatiently to be introduced.

"Sarah, this is Ryan's friend, Max." My voice is a bit wobbly.

Max slides into a seat at the end of our table and points at my cheek saying, "Quite something you got there."

"Oh, it's nothing," I say.

Max's face crinkles into a grin. He's really nice looking. I hadn't noticed on Sunday. He's long and thin and his eyes are a bright sky-blue and really huge. He's wearing a black jacket, which looks well worn, and outdoorsy trousers, and he has the longest, thinnest fingers I've ever seen.

"You two know each other from school?" says Max.

"When she goes," says Sar, giving me a frown.

"I'm too sick to go to school," I say and roll my eyes.

Max laughs. "I didn't have that excuse so I made up a sick granny I had to visit all the time."

"Nice one," says Sarah. "My parents would find out if I didn't go, so I go every day." She sighs. "It's tough but someone has to do it."

I give her a push. "You love it. She has a heavy social life to maintain."

"Party girl," says Max.

He looks about the same age as Ryan, seventeen, maybe eighteen. He's more self-assured and definitely not a student. I can see he's smitten.

"So what do you do if you don't go to school?" Sarah asks him.

"I work at my Dad's camping shop round the corner. But what I really do is climb."

"Climb what?" says Sarah.

"Mountains," he says. "I'm aiming for Everest."

"Wow!" Sarah's impressed. I'm glad because he's Ryan's friend and a love interest might distract her from my problems at the moment. I don't know how long I can keep this secret from her anyway, but maybe things will get sorted before I have to come clean.

Or I'll be in Africa. Either way, I think I'll leave these two alone, so I make my excuses. "Well kiddies," I say, "I have to run, got a scan."

Sarah gives me a grateful look. Max's huge eyes are fixed on her so my timing's perfect.

"I'm ringing you tonight," Sar calls after me as I head for the door.

I don't turn round. Hopefully Max will help her to forget that promise. I need some space to think.

Chapter 12

Ryan

So far, it's been an awful week. Lee sent me a million texts on Monday and Tuesday. Tuesday night, she said she'd tell her Dad if I didn't come over. I can't take time off, and if I miss work, Shelley says she'll sack me: not done my six months probation yet. So it's seven fifteen on Wednesday morning and I'm driving to Portsmouth. I've never driven this far before. But Dad does it in twenty minutes. I'm aiming to be back and at work by nine.

No way can I lose my job, too. I need money, shedloads. All I've got in the bank is four hundred and I need a hundred to buy the jeans to sell on the road trip. Otherwise I'll get to Africa and I won't be able to get back.

"They don't deport you from Nigeria, man," Olu told me. "They cannot afford the air fares. They just put you in prison and forget about you, oh boy." And he shakes his hand again. I never know what to believe when Olu talks about Nigeria, but I can't risk it.

The road to Portsmouth is jam-packed. Hadn't reckoned on rush hour. I'm not even sure the camper will get that far. There's a sort of shake, which Dad says is the timing and we still haven't got it right. And what if it overheats?

Somehow I make it to the turn-off to town but I get totally lost behind the football ground. Lee said her road was between a row of shops and a garage but I keep turning down dead ends. Then a refuse lorry comes in behind me and I'm stuck for ages.

In the end I pull the camper onto a forecourt and ring Lee. She gives me more directions and what feels like hours later I finally turn into her road. What a journey! I'll never get back to work on time.

Lee's in her front garden, hanging off the gate. When I pull up and get out of the van she flings herself at me like a little kid. Before I can say anything a huge motorbike roars up, skids to a halt and the rider pulls off his crash helmet.

"Who's this then?" says the bloke.

Must be Lee's Dad, and he doesn't look friendly.

"A friend from school," says Lee.

"I'm Ryan," I say politely and hold out my hand.

"Wayne," he says, ignoring the hand.

He's wearing leathers and his hair sticks up in crazy tufts like horns. He's got the angriest eyes I've ever seen.

Wayne pulls something off the back of his bike, something long and thin wrapped in a green cloth, and walks off into the house.

"He's been out shooting," Lee says.

"You what?"

"That's his hobby. Shooting things. Rabbits, birds, other stuff, you know. He's got a locked cellar full of guns. Shotguns, handguns, even old guns from the war. He goes out before work."

God! I couldn't have picked a worse person to cross. I'm dead.

"Does he know about, you know...." I nod towards her middle.

She shakes her head. She's playing with the latch on the gate, flicking it up and down.

"What about your Mum?" It's annoying that she won't look at me.

She shrugs again. "It's just me and Dad, Mum went off with another bloke two years ago."

"And you stayed with your Dad?"

"He's OK when you get to know him."

"But not so OK that you can tell him you're pregnant?" I point out.

"No way. He'd kill...."

"Me?"

She nods and I have a vision of her Dad skidding up to our house on his bike with a pump action rifle and taking out the whole family in a tsunami of blood.

"We can't talk here," I say. It's already eight and I'll have to set off again soon.

"Park?"

I nod and we walk off. Lee's very quiet and she's skipping along beside me. Me and Max used to take his little sister to the park. She'd skip along, singing to herself. But Lee is sixteen, only a year younger than me.

I glance over; I haven't really looked at her much before. Her hair's tied back in a pink band. She's wearing a hooded sweatshirt and jeans with trainers. Jess wouldn't be seen dead in pink or trainers.

When we get to the park we sit on a bench and I ask,

"How do you know you're pregnant?"

"Test."

"You seen a doctor?"

She shakes her head.

"How do you know it's mine?"

This has been doing my head in. Maybe she sleeps with every bloke she meets. Maybe it's someone else's. Maybe she isn't even pregnant.

"There isn't anyone else," she says in a small voice. Her eyes fill with tears and I know she's telling the truth. My heart sinks.

"Why did you, you know?"

"Do it with you?" she asks and I nod. "For a dare. What about you?"

I don't say anything. I can't tell her it was because my little brother teased me for being a virgin, can I?

"I thought you had to be experienced to get pregnant," she says, and she starts to cry.

I don't know what to do when girls cry. I've had even less experience at that. But I put my arm round her and say, "Don't worry, it'll be OK. We'll work it out."

I can't help thinking that this is all James's fault. I hate him so much. I'm planning my revenge on him when Lee sniffs back her tears and blows her nose.

"It's not too late," she says.

"What for?"

"You know, they do it for you if it's less than twenty-four weeks."

I don't know what she means. "Do what?"

The park is beginning to fill up with kids and their mums. It's one of those damp leafy days when it's not really cold. Good day for working under the van; I imagine the feel of grease between my fingers.

"Get rid of it. Abortion."

Oh God!

"Is that what you want?" I ask and for a minute I think she's going to say yes. You have to pay for them. I could take all my money out of the cash machine right now and give it to her. I'd be free to go to Africa and she wouldn't have to tell her Dad and we could all get back to normal. I could get back to Jessica Fitzgerald.

"I don't know," she says. "What do you want?"

It's the biggest question anyone ever asked me in my entire life. I feel like the balance of the universe lies in my hands and it feels terrifying and amazing and totally impossible all at once.

I say the only thing I *can* say, "I'll go with whatever you decide." Did I just sign my own death warrant?

All the way home in the van my head's whirling round and round. Should I have said, get rid of it? Should I have driven her to the cash machine, given her my money and said, never contact me again?

Lee is nothing compared to Jess. How could I have got her pregnant after just one time? I'm carrying condoms strapped to my body for the rest of my life.

Africa, Africa, Africa goes round and round my head for the last mile; I'm almost chanting it as I get home. The first person I see on the drive is James with his arm draped round Pippa's shoulders.

I look at his smug face out of the window and give him a look of the most poisonous hatred I can muster. I almost wrench the handbrake out at the roots as I park.

He just gives me the finger and steers Pippa down the road, their school bags swinging as he laughs his head off.

I clench the steering wheel until my knuckles go white.

Chapter 13

By the time I get the van home and catch the bus back to work, I'm already late. Shelley will go mad, but I don't really care. I haven't seen Jess since Sunday. Three whole days. Maybe she's gone off me after they way I was at the oyster beds. Should I ring her before I go into work? I still remember the feel of her lips on mine. When we parted I thought we were OK. Only I didn't tell her about Lee and the baby.

I've got to see Max; I can't cope with all this on my own anymore.

The bus stops on the High Street and I walk over to the camping shop. Max will know what to do, even if he goes mad at me. But when I get to the shop he's already left for Brighton, picking up new stock with his Dad. I walk out feeling like I'm carrying all the pebbles from the beach on my back.

As I go over to the hospital my phone rings. It's Jess.

"Meet in the burger bar after work today?"

Yesss! But my next thought is about Lee and the baby. What should I do? Should I tell Jess? So she knows what she's getting into?

"Ryan?" she says.

Would it be unfair to see her without telling her? Lee and me haven't made any decisions, and I really want to see Jess, see if Sunday was real.

"Yes. Great," I say, and there's a little sigh before she clicks off.

As I walk through the hospital, phone in my hand, I think about sending Mum a text telling her the whole story. I plan it in my head, **got girl pregnant. terrified. help,** and I start to tap it out, but I stop at the end of **preg** and stare at the screen feeling a mounting panic. There's got to be a better way than this. Max'll know, Max has an answer for everything. I've pointed this out to him before.

"It's the climbing," he says. "Once you've hung upside down defying gravity a hundred feet up a rock face you can find a solution to most things."

I've never defied death. I have no life experience to prepare me for anything, let alone this.

Shelley's a nightmare all day. I nearly quit. Only I can't. I need the money for the baby. And Africa. I can't give up on Africa. Maybe Jess will come with me. On Sunday, she sounded desperate to get away from her blockhead Dad. I like that word. My brother is a total blockhead. Look what he's pushed me into.

Lee and I aren't going to decide anything until next week. We need some space to get our heads round everything, but what should I say to Jess tonight?

Shelley makes me work until after six, which is much later than usual. By the time I get to the burger bar Jess is already sitting there with a box of chicken and chips.

She looks up when I come in and her eyes flicker a little and then she smiles.

"Hey," I say and slide onto the seat opposite her.

For once I don't say anything stupid. I just take a chip

and put it in my mouth.

"Guess what?" she says.

"What?"

"Max and Sarah have hooked up."

I take another chip and say, "Who?"

"Sarah, my best friend, and Max, your best friend."

"How?"

"They met in Starbucks yesterday. Sar and me were chatting and Max walked in and I just left them to it. She texted me to say they are going out tonight."

"Nice one," I say.

"We'll have to double date," she says and she giggles like a girl. I mean she *is* a girl, of course, but she's usually so sad and serious. I've never seen her like this before.

"That'll be a first," I say.

"We could have a beach party," says Jess.

"In November?"

"OK, maybe not, but there's a pyjama party next weekend."

"Except I wear pants in bed," I say and then I blush.

But Jess laughs. A big, full-on laugh, and then she eats a whole chicken wing. I've never seen her eat so much.

"You know on Sunday," I start, not sure how to carry on. I'm eyeing her warily but she just nods and licks her fingers, "I was a bit, you know, off. It wasn't anything to do with you – you know that don't you?"

She picks up another chicken wing, turns it over and puts it down again. I'm holding my breath, sitting very still, waiting for the axe to fall.

"So what was it then?" she says finally.

"Blockhead stuff," I say, because I know she'll understand what I mean.

"I've had blockhead squared all week." She grins at me. "I'm sick of it."

It feels so good that we've got something in common, even though we're not big on detail. But it feels like we're a team, a pair, an item.

"So what do you want to do?" I say.

"I want to see your van properly and I want you to tell me about Africa."

Awesome.

We catch the bus back across the bridge onto the Island and get off at the village shop. Everyone's home by now but I don't care. I take Jess's hand as we walk up the path and I keep hold of it while I fumble for my key, open the front door, let us both in and shut it behind us. Still holding hands I lead her down the hall and into the kitchen.

Mum is yelling at James, "What do you mean, weekend detention? What on earth have you been up to? It's that girlfriend. I don't like her, with her fancy ways and her Dad driving around in that Merc...."

"Like a drug dealer," Dad cuts in.

James is leaning against the sink, hands stuffed in the pockets of his school trousers, head bent. His shirt is hanging out and the buttons are done up wrong. He looks about ten.

"Mum, Dad, this is Jess. Can she stay to tea?"

James looks up and his mouth drops open. I give him a big smug smirk.

You blockhead, I think.

Mum's face breaks into a polite smile and she says, "Of course love, you sit here, Jess," and she fusses round, flicking a tea towel at James and sending him out of the kitchen to clean up.

"What's he been up to now?" I say, like a proper eldest son.

"Selling kisses from his girlfriend for a pound a piece," says Dad. "What a pair."

Jess and I exchange grins and she tucks her hair behind her ears.

I sit down next to Jess and Dad sits down at the head of the table and Mum starts dishing up soup as though we've been expected. It's never been like this. Me and a girlfriend just popping in, casual like, for dinner. By the time James comes down in a scruffy old T-shirt and jeans, which are too short for him, we're all chatting.

No one looks up as he takes his seat opposite me and Jess. Jess has her hand on the table and I cover it with my hand, turn her face towards me and kiss her lightly on the lips.

James doesn't even dare snort.

Chapter 14

Jess

Jess Jayne Fitzgerald see everyone in school tomorrow!
Sarah Jayne Lewis yaaaay ☺☺
Hello Kitty sooo much to tell you hunii
Alix Miller excellent
Emily Jayne Brown wish i was there hate my new school all geeks – missing you guys sooo much and whos ryan??????????!!!!!!!!!!!!!!!
Jess Jayne Fitzgerald ☺

On Friday I decide to go into school and see everyone. My face doesn't look too bad and for once I haven't got a hospital appointment.

First lesson is Business Studies. That used to be my favourite subject because of Dad wanting me to go into the business.

Mr Bennett smiles at me in a nice way when I go in. "Good to see you, Jess, got your coursework?"

I don't even answer; I'm never doing coursework again.

I've pretty much decided I'm going to Africa with Ryan. Dad is hardly at home anymore. It's almost two weeks since the wallets and he promised to sort everything out. But he's broken all his promises and he lies to Mum about business meetings all over the place. I can't keep up the pretence much longer; sometimes I think it's going to burst out of me.

I asked Mum for some lunch money at breakfast. I wanted to see what she would say. She gave me a bit of a funny look and then she pulled the charity tin down from the top shelf and took out three pound coins.

I raised an eyebrow and she said, "Your Dad forgot to go to the cash machine."

She *must* be getting suspicious. When will she say something?

"I'll need your piece on the Euro by next week, Jess," says Mr Bennett, and he's walking round the room, dropping folders onto desks.

In your dreams, I think.

Lunch break is great. Everyone crowds round asking me about Ryan. Sarah told everyone over Facebook.

"He sounds so hot," says Billie. She's Hello Kitty on Facebook. She loves Hello Kitty.

"He is," says Sarah, and she's got her arm linked through mine.

We met up at Max's last night, me and Ryan and Max and Sar, after dinner at Ryan's house. Ryan drove us in the van and we sang along to cheesy ABBA songs all the way.

Max sent out for Chinese and opened some cans. We'd already eaten at Ryan's, but I had a beer and a spoonful of rice with a square of chicken and Ryan was really pleased with me. I don't mind eating a bit when I'm with Ryan.

"You'll get better if you start eating properly," he said.

"He's a right proper medic, ain't you mate?" Max said.

Ryan went red and he looked so sweet.

The playground is getting more crowded and Sarah pulls

me to the benches under the trees. Billie, Sarah and I sit and chat and giggle and it feels really good to be normal with them. We see Alix Miller coming over with Samir; they're such a weird couple.

Sarah snickers and says, "Here comes your Social Worker." She exchanges looks with Billie. But I feel a bit uncomfortable.

Alix means well but she's not in our gang.

"Did you get the Science notes?" Alix says.

The others laugh but I feel a bit mean. And let's face it, I'm going to need all the friends I can get when everyone finds out about my Dad. I can hardly look Sarah in the face when I think about it. What will the bank do when they find out about the fraud? What will her Dad do? Even if I'm a thousand miles away, driving through Africa, I won't be able to escape. The world's a small place now everyone's on Facebook.

So I say, "Yes, thanks a lot. Appreciate it."

"No probs," says Alix, and she and Samir smile at me and wander off.

Sar gives me a look but I pretend I don't see. She has no idea what's coming.

After school we all go to Starbucks. I text Ryan to see if he can take a break so I can show him off. But he doesn't even text back. That means psycho Shelley is on his case.

"You have to come to school Monday," says Billie, sucking on a milkshake.

"Two days in a row?" I say.

"No, you have to," says Sarah. "It's Danny's birthday."

"Danny Fisher?"

"Yeah, and you know what that means?"

We all exchange looks, then we scream-laugh. Last year Danny smuggled two bottles of vodka into school on his birthday. Half the class squeezed into the games cupboard, which is like a small room. Sar and me were crushed up against Greg and Keith Best, who are both hot. The bottles kept going round and round and everyone was swigging and laughing and snogging. We were off our heads by the afternoon and then we had P.E. with Minty Jones, who's a bit dim and didn't seem to realise.

"You all seem in a good mood today. What did you have for lunch?" he asked in his I'm-one-of-you voice.

"Danny didn't have no lunch, did you mate?" yelled out Greg, and Keith gave him a shove.

We persuaded Minty to let us do mixed football. It was completely crazy, with the girls picking up the ball and running in all directions and the boys blowing them kisses when they caught them up. Danny and Keith passed out in the goal mouth, face down, practically eating mud.

"OK," I say, grinning. "Can't miss Danny's birthday, can I?"

The rest of the day passes quite nicely, but I'm really tired by the time I get home. Mum and Veeve are in the living room watching a soap. I go upstairs and lie on my bed. It was great being with everyone at school and having a laugh together. I'll miss them when I go away.

fri nov 21
I wasn't sure about Ryan after his mood last Sunday. But we've had such nice times since then. I'm one hundred per cent sure he's the right boy for me. He knows I've been ill and he doesn't care. I've got a great boyfriend, we're going to Africa and Dad and Mum can sort out their own stuff. Not my problem!!!

I'm so tired after my first day in school for ages that I fall asleep as soon as I've changed out of my uniform, waking up when I hear the front door slam. It's pitch dark outside my window and my clock says seven. I must have slept for two hours.

I hear Dad calling out to Mum and Veeve downstairs and their voices answering. They all sound in such a good mood. I decide to go down and see what's for dinner; maybe Dad has some good news for me.

When I go into the kitchen everyone's in there and I'm just about to say hi when I see Veeve has her hand out and Dad's counting ten pound notes into her palm.

I'm so shocked to see him with money again, after everything he's said and done, I can't help myself.

"What are you doing?" I almost shout. Even if things are a bit better, surely Dad can't afford that much pocket money yet?

Mum is on the phone but she takes it away from her ear and they all stare at me as if I've gone mad. I feel like a stranger in the house again. Who are these people? Why do I live with them? Maybe *this* is the moment when they tell me I'm adopted.

"Dad's just giving me some money for the weekend," says Veeve as if it's the most natural thing in the world.

"You can't do that!" I say. "Are you mad?"

"You're the mad one," mutters Veeve. "Jealous cow."

I can't believe this. Dad's glaring at me, his eyebrows arched into a horrid point.

Mum lifts her hand and points a newly manicured nail at me. "What is the *matter* with you these days?"

I wonder how much that manicure cost.

Dad says, "Come on now Jess, love—" but I don't let him finish.

I put my hand out and snap, "Give me your credit card!"

Chapter 15

"Really Jess, you're getting so cheeky, especially towards your Dad." Mum breaks off texting and glares at me.

Veeve lets out a high-pitched giggle.

Do my family care about me now I'm not dying on a cancer ward? I keep my eyes fixed on Dad. He stares back, unflinching.

"Give me the card," I say rudely again. "I'm going shopping with Sarah in the morning. I need a new ski jacket for the trip. Give me the card you got this cash out with."

Where did he get that cash for Veeve? There must be fifty pounds in her hand now. Who could he be stealing from? Or has he tried the stolen credit card again? If so, he must have taken out hundreds if he's giving Veeve that much.

Veeve's right when she says I'm jealous. I am insanely jealous because she's being protected from the truth and I'm suffering. Again. Just like when I was in hospital.

Dad's eyes begin to narrow. He's been lending me his card since I was fourteen. I never forget the pin or lose it. He looks like a cornered animal, his shoulders hunched, chin stuck out.

"Have you changed the pin number?" I say. "Or is it still 4536, yours and Mum's ages last birthday?" I'm almost spitting at him.

To my amazement he says, "OK, Jess, but you could have asked me more politely," and he starts thumbing through his wallet. He pulls out a supermarket loyalty card and carefully slots it back in.

He looks thoughtful for a few seconds and then he says, "Oh, I forgot, I changed the pin this week and I can't for the life of me remember it. I'm waiting for them to send me a new pin through the post."

Very clever, I think.

"2439," says Veeve with a grin on her face.

"What?" says Dad, and I see a bead of sweat appear on his forehead.

"We'll guess," says Mum grinning, and she and Veeve start firing numbers rapidly.

Dad laughs and holds up his hand. "Whoa, family! You only get three guesses anyway!"

All three of them are lined up in front of the sink, exchanging grins and enjoying a joke together as though this was a normal happy family without a care in the world. The room does a spin and my head feels like it's going to burst. My fingers close round a wine glass on the table. One of Mum's best glasses.

Mum's looking at me and looking at the glass. It's about half-full with red wine. I pick up the glass and gulp down the wine. It goes straight to my head and it's as though a hot wave has swept right through me.

"You've no right," I say, and then I raise my arm and throw the glass onto the floor. It smashes with a crashing sound. We have quarry tiles, so everything breaks the second you drop it.

They all jump and Mum goes quite white. She opens her mouth to say something and I cut her off.

"Give me the card!" I scream and it's as though I can't stop now.

There are plates on the table. I pick one up and throw it against a cupboard. They all duck and I smash another plate on the floor. There aren't any more plates in reach so I bend down to pick up a broken piece to throw again and I'm shaking so much I cut my hand. Blood drips onto the floor but I can't feel anything except this massive anger.

"I want the card!" I scream.

I can't seem to stop. Over and over I'm screaming, "Give me the card, I want the card!"

Is this what it's like to go insane? They'll probably call the doctor and I'll get locked up when they should be locking my Dad up!

No one moves, as if they're all frozen in shock.

Then Dad lifts his hand and says, "Steady on, Jessie love," but I'm sure I see a look of pure evil in his eyes.

"I hate you!" I yell.

Veeve lets out a gasp but nothing can stop me now.

"I hate your face and your eyes and your mouth and your smell, I hate your stinky feet and your hairy hands. I'm not your daughter anymore, I don't belong in this house, in this family, in this town, on this planet." My voice cracks up with the pressure and I stop.

There's a horrified silence.

Then, without looking at any of them, I run out the kitchen, down the hall, wrench open the front door and run down the path to the street. I keep on running and running, my legs aching because I haven't run anywhere for months, my lungs burning as they try to keep up.

It's pouring with rain, huge freezing sheets of water blow in off the sea. I'm drenched in minutes. I'm only wearing an old sweatshirt but it has a hood. I pull it up but it's soon soaked through. My jeans are soaking from the bottoms up. They drag on the ground because I'm wearing pumps, and my feet, with no socks, are soaked and going numb.

I stop running and I'm stumbling along, crying and crying. Where can I go, who will help me? I can't go to Sarah because of her bank manager Dad. And I can't go to Nana Hat because it might kill her to see me insane.

Mad people behave like this, don't they? Look what I've just done; smashed up the kitchen, said horrible things, run off in the rain. What if everyone turns against me now, and what if Nana Hat doesn't love me anymore? It's not fair, this isn't my fault, Dad has to tell them now.

I stumble along in the dark and the rain, telling myself that's what will happen. Dad will confess everything and explain why I've been so rude for the past two weeks, and especially tonight. Then he'll come looking for me because he'll be worried I'll get sick again out here in the rain and the dark. Florence Mum will be worried too. The doctors said I had to be very careful this winter. My immune system is very low because of the illness. I could catch all sorts of germs. It could go to my chest. Mum will want me home as soon as possible, won't she?

I see the bus shelter up ahead. I go under it and sit down

on the tiny hard seats. The rain is blowing in horizontally now and I'm shaking with cold and soaked right through. Water is pouring off my head and trickling down the back of my neck. It's so cold, it's like torture.

I decide I'll sit here and wait for Dad. I can't walk all the way home in this. He'll come and get me and cuddle me and take me home and tell me everything is fine, it was all a big mistake and he's got plenty of money and he hasn't stolen anything else.

But no one comes.

A bus pulls in and then pulls out again.

Then I see a man turn the corner and I can't see who it is. Is it Dad?

Then I realise I'm scared, I'm absolutely terrified.

What if it is Dad? Look what happened when I caught him at the cash machine. I've still got the bruise. He's really angry with me now, he might think I'm going to the police and he's come out not to find me and take me home, but to stop me. Or hurt me. Then a thought occurs to me. What if it's not Dad? I start to shake, more with fear than from the cold.

There's nowhere to hide, I crunch myself up as small as I can in the bus shelter and hope the man will just go past. I'm too scared to look. The wind's howling and howling and rain's lashing against the shelter. I can't even hear footsteps on the pavement and then a voice says, "You got the time?"

I look up. It isn't Dad. It's a man, a strange-looking man, leering at me in a horrible way. I'm out here all by myself in the dark. Oh God!

"No," I say.

Then the most wonderful sound in the world starts up. The James Bond theme tune, the ring tone on Nana Hat's old mobile. I dig in my pocket.

The man turns and sloshes off through the rain.

It's Ryan.

"Hey," he says, and I feel hot tears begin to fall down my face, mixing with the freezing rain. "What's up?"

"Nothing," I say, but he can hear my voice is breaking. "Where are you?"

"Bus shelter near my house."

"But it's raining." He sounds worried. Someone's actually worried about me.

I start sobbing and he says, "Stay there, Jess, just stay there, I'm coming to get you."

My Dad's left me out in the rain to be raped, murdered and dumped on the beach like that sixteen-year-old in Southsea last month. My boyfriend is coming to rescue me because he cares about me.

We should leave for Africa tomorrow.

Chapter 16

Ryan

I'm stuck with James until Sunday. Mum and Dad have gone up to London for the weekend to see the uncles and go to a show. They do it every year and usually me and James stay over with friends.

"You can look after things this year, can't you love?" Mum said to me a couple of weeks ago. I just shrugged and said, of course. But that was before I found out about Lee, and wanted to kill James for pushing me into the biggest mistake of my life.

I can't stop thinking about babies. I see them everywhere now: in the hospital, in the street when I go for lunch, there was even one in the camping shop this morning.

I still haven't told Max. He's got a new girlfriend, Jess's best mate, Sarah. We've hung out as a foursome – we had Chinese and beers at Max's place, so things are even more complicated now.

If I tell Max he'll tell Sarah and then she'll tell Jess.

Mum and Dad left at about six. They left us money to get pizza and James ordered. He knows I hate anchovies so he got extra. I'd go out and get chips, but there's a terrible storm. The branches on the trees in the front garden have been banging against the windows all evening.

"Pippa's coming over at eight," he says, flicking TV

channels with the volume turned right up to drown out the noise of the rain. "You having Jess over?"

"What's it to you?" I growl and James gives his smug little grin. I hadn't thought about asking her over, but maybe I will. It's all good with us. She said she really wants to come on the road trip with me. Do we have any future though? The baby's not going to disappear, however far we drive. I push the thought away.

I wonder if Jess has asked her parents about Africa. I mentioned snakes but she didn't seem bothered, not like me. She's not sixteen until December. I don't even know if she's got a passport.

I call her to ask and she answers straight away. She's in a right state, sobbing down the phone at me. She's outside in some bus shelter and I can hear the storm blowing down the phone.

"I'm coming," I say. "Hang on."

James is looking over at me nervously as I'm talking on the phone.

"I've got to go and pick Jess up," I say.

Thing is, James might be a cocky little jerk about women but he hates being in the house on his own. He's scared of the dark, has been since he was little. I'm not the only one with phobias in this family.

"Don't be long," he says.

"I'm on my mobile, all right, mate?"

He nods and follows me to the door and I hear him lock it and put the chain on behind me.

He'll be OK. Mum would kill me if anything happened, but Jess is crying and sitting out in the rain.

I can't believe the state of her when I find her at the bus shelter. She's completely soaked and shivering. She flings herself on me and sobs about her Dad and how she hates him and she can never go home. I bundle her in the van and drive her back and James, for once, doesn't say anything, just gets a towel and puts the kettle on.

She can't seem to stop shaking and crying and she's cut her hand.

"Come up close to the gas fire," I say, and I pull the red blanket off the back of the sofa and tuck it round her.

She's stopped crying now but she's still shivering. "Could I have a tissue?" she says in a small voice.

"Course, yes, I'll find some."

Mum usually has a box of tissues in the kitchen. When I go in James is dunking a tea bag in a mug. "So your girlfriend's here, after all," he says, shaking his head in mock surprise.

"You can see the state she's in," I snarl.

"I'm just saying."

"Well don't. She's in trouble so be nice."

James stirs milk into the mug and says, "Pippa's not coming now, her Dad won't drive her."

One less problem to worry about. I pick up the tissue box and go back into the living room.

"Mum's got a first aid box in the bathroom," I say to Jess, unsure about leaving her again, but she gives me a slight nod. She looks quite sleepy in front of the warm fire.

As I take the stairs two at a time I think about how she

had that mark on her face last week and now a cut hand. I wonder if her Dad knocks her about? Is that why she hates him so much? I feel a surge of anger go through me and I clench my fists. How could he, her being so ill and everything?

Back downstairs Jess lets me look at the cut.

"It looks quite deep," I say, wishing Max was here. Should I take her to casualty for stitches? "Does it hurt?"

"It's OK. Just stick a plaster on it," she says, but she winces when I cover it.

James comes in carrying a tray with the mug of tea and a slice of pizza he's warmed up in the microwave. "It's hot," he says.

"Thanks," says Jess.

"There's plenty more. My girlfriend can't come over."

"Sorry," says Jess. "I hope it's not because of me."

"Nah. Anyhow I see her all the time."

Show off, I think.

"Are you warm enough?" I say to Jess as we settle on the sofa. Our knees are almost touching and I feel embarrassed in front of James, because it's just the three of us.

Her lips are blue, and her fingers, gripping the mug, are dead white.

She nods and sips her tea.

James is flicking channels again and finds a repeat of Doctor Who: it's the Christmas special from two years ago.

"This all right?" he says and I nod.

Who cares what we watch? We can't talk with James

here and I don't want to invite her upstairs to my bedroom, although that would be the best place. Not because it's a bedroom, with a bed and all that of course. Only that I think it would scare Jessica Fitzgerald tonight.

And I need to figure out what's happened and how this affects everything else, Africa and us and the baby. Everything comes back to the baby.

Then the doorbell goes. It's Max.

"All right, mate? What's up?" He's got Sarah with him and he's got his arm round her as we go down the hall and into the living room.

When she sees Jess, Sarah says, "I've been trying to ring you!"

Jess goes even more pale if that's possible. She can't meet Sarah's eye. So whatever's happened, she doesn't want Sarah to know.

"Just having a quiet one here this weekend," she says.

James throws her a surprised look but he doesn't speak.

There's an awkward silence and then Max says in his cheery voice, "Why don't you come with us? We're off to the Roaches."

Max is always going on about the climbing at the Roaches – it's meant to be the best rock climbing in England.

He says things like, "You should have seen Jonno on the Vice last Sunday," then he has to explain that the Vice is one of the climbs in the handbook and it's vicious. Max only made it for the first time this summer.

I don't fancy it.

We all stare at him and he's looking from one face to the next and then he says, "Don't all cheer at once."

"We're actually doing something," I say, shooting James a warning look.

But then Jess says in a rush, "No we're not. We'll come."

"What?" I say.

"Let's go. I want to, Ryan, I really want to."

"I'm not staying here on my own," James says, and his eyes go wide.

"That's all right, mate, you can come too. Got my Dad's old Galaxy for the weekend, seven seater," says Max as if that decides everything.

"Hang on," I say. "We can't just take off. What about Mum and Dad and the house and...."

"No!" Jess almost shouts. Everyone stares at her and she stretches her mouth into a smile but I can see it's a big effort. "It'll be...." she's searching for the right word, "....fun."

It's then I realise. Jess wants to get away from here. It's not only me who has a secret. Jessica Fitzgerald has a secret too and I'll put money on it being something to do with her Dad knocking her about. Like me, Jess wants to ... no, *needs to*, run away. She's clinging on to the offer of this weekend like a climber on the edge of a rock face.

But the thought of spending the weekend with other people makes me feel trapped. I just want to be on my own to think. And now there's Jess's secret too. How are we going to keep our secrets from everyone for an entire weekend?

The nightmare begins here.

Chapter 17

Max insists we leave tonight.

"We can be in the climber's hut before midnight," he says. "Make the most of the weekend."

Sarah says she has enough clothes to share with Jess. "Tell your parents you're sleeping over at mine."

"OK," says Jess with a girly giggle, pretending she hasn't a care in the world. Sarah doesn't seem to have noticed that Jess is probably being battered by her Dad.

James has slung some stuff in his school backpack and he's waiting by the door.

It's still raining when we go out to the Galaxy. There are three rows of seats. Max has all his climbing gear piled in the back and he makes James sit there.

"Don't you girls want to sit together?" he says as Jess gets in the middle row.

"No," says Jess and pulls me in next to her.

Sarah gives Max a shove and says with a giggle, "They want cuddle-up time."

Max slams the doors and James starts protesting he's squashed in with all the gear.

"Shut it," I snap, "or we'll leave you behind."

Then my phone goes. It's Lee calling. Oh God.

"Phone," says Max as he fires up the engine and takes off down the road. He's in such a good mood. He should know what's in my head: Jess with her maniac Dad, Lee with her psycho Dad, the baby. Africa feels as though it's slipping through my fingers like Sahara sand.

My Dad wants me to settle down after the road trip, get a trade, become a mechanic or something. How can I do any of that with a baby? I'll end up in a supermarket, stacking shelves – and living in a dump.

I keep imagining Mum's face when I tell her.

"You've been so foolish, Ryan," she'll say. She'll be so disappointed.

The ring tone's still blaring on my phone.

"Phone," says Max again. "Is someone going to answer that?"

"It's no one," I mutter and press to ignore the call. A couple of minutes later I get a text. I take a quick squint at Jess. She's staring out of the window, her body half turned away from me.

"How many girlfriends you got, mate?" says Max.

"You serious?" James yells from the back of the car.

Sarah twists round, trying to catch Jess's eye, but Jess ignores her. She's cradling her wounded hand in her lap and it looks as though the plaster's leaking blood.

Max puts on the radio and a steady beat fills the van. It's dark outside and still raining. There's nothing to see but Jess keeps her face glued to the window.

I check the text. It's from Lee. call me. dads on my back. sooo lonly ☹

I press the delete button quickly.

It takes hours to get to Derbyshire. We stop once at a

motorway services and I buy the snacks. Well I have to, don't I? Jess doesn't seem to have any cash with her and Max is doing all the driving. James takes advantage and has burger, chips and a coke. I don't yell at him – we're in public, and I'd look a right idiot. Sarah and Max have doughnuts and coffee and Jess has a bottle of water.

It comes to fifteen pounds. I'm in shock. That's almost three hours' pay, and Shelley's cutting overtime from Monday. But the climber's hut is free, Max has brought all the gear and he says he doesn't want anything for petrol, so it's still a cheap weekend. He's my best mate.

I'm so desperate to talk to him about Lee that I follow him into the bogs, but there's a line up of footie fans along the urinal. Max starts chatting about Sarah and asking me stuff about Jess. I just mumble back.

Back on the motorway, I get a load of texts from Lee, all at once. I must have been out of signal before.

"Someone loves you," says Sarah with a giggle.

"It's just spam," I mutter, silencing it quickly.

"Turn it off," says Max.

I can't answer Lee now I've said it's spam, and what if Jess can see my screen? But if I don't answer she might get desperate and tell her Dad. In the end I say I'm going to text Mum and send a text to Lee: **battery dying ring u tomoz.**

Then I put my phone on silent, muttering something about Mum expecting to keep in touch with us, but I feel like chucking it out the window.

We arrive at the climber's hut at about midnight. There's already a bunch of students there and they've taken most of the bunks. There's only one room in the whole place.

"You're kidding," I say to Max as we bring in our sleeping bags. I have to sleep here with Jess? And James!

"Don't worry, mate," says Max cheerfully. "They're climbers. Very respectful. You'll see."

James claims a bottom bunk near the wall. I feel a bit responsible for him, as he is the youngest here. So I go over and say, "You OK?"

He gives me a grin and says, "Now's your big chance to do it, push a couple of bunks together."

I almost raise my fist to him. He's already screwed up my entire life once. Isn't that enough? But Sarah calls me over to help her with the bags from the car.

Once we get back inside I see Jess laying out her stuff. She's got us a couple of bottom bunks next to each other, and they are pushed together quite close. Sarah and Max have taken the two on top of us and I can already hear them whispering.

I go over just as one of the climbers yells, "Lights out."

The room goes dark and there are cheers and boos all round. I take advantage, slip off my jeans and dive quickly into my sleeping bag before Jess's eyes can adjust and she sees my boxers.

Someone says, "First one up in the morning gets tea in bed for everyone."

"You what?" calls out Sarah.

"Club hut tradition, sweetheart," and there are more laughs.

The bunks shake as everyone settles down and then I feel something warm on my shoulder through my sleeping bag.

I pull my hand out and meet Jess's hand, reaching across from her bunk.

"Sorry, Ryan," she says in a small voice.

"What for?" I'm the one who should be saying sorry.

"I know you didn't want to come, but there was so much blockhead stuff at home. I had to get away. Sorry."

I can't think of anything to say. I'm the blockhead. So I just mutter, "Hey."

"Hey," she says back and then she's silent, fallen asleep, exhausted probably.

I lie awake all night worrying and worrying and worrying.

Chapter 18
Jess

It's freezing out here. No one else seems to notice. James is so sweet, he gave me his Liverpool scarf but I wish I had my furry jacket with the hood. Sar doesn't feel the cold so much. She's just got a jumper on over her jeans.

"Layer up, you'll be fine," she said this morning while the students were frying eggs.

I pulled on everything I could but the wind cuts straight through.

I can't believe what's happened since yesterday. If Ryan knew the truth would he dump me? He hasn't asked me how I cut my hand but he's given me some funny looks. He's getting suspicious, I'm sure. What would he say if I told him my Dad's a criminal and I'm insane? That I threw a load of plates at my family and smashed the kitchen up before running off.

It was such a bad drive up here last night. Ryan was in a right mood and his phone kept going off. I couldn't help wondering who it was, even though he said it was spam.

I turned my phone off once Ryan picked me up from the bus stop, didn't want to speak to Mum or anyone. But when we were in the car I felt a bit guilty and switched it on. There were about a dozen missed calls, voice mails and texts, all from Mum. That felt good, but nothing from Veeve or Dad, which made me feel both angry and sad.

I was just about to send a text when my phone rang.

It was Mum. "Jess? Where on earth are you? It's such a terrible night. Veeve took the car and came out looking for you. Jess?"

So Dad wasn't worried about me.

"Jess? Answer me," she'd pleaded.

Her voice had got more and more ratty; she was probably late for cocktails with the girls. I almost switched the phone off but I was scared she might ring Nana Hat. I don't want *her* to worry about me.

"I'm at Sar's," I'd said.

"Oh," Mum said. "Well ... if her parents don't mind. What on earth was all that screaming about? You made a terrible mess! Your Dad had to clear it up."

Good, I'd thought. I hope he cuts himself and bleeds to death. But then I got a stab of guilt in the abdomen: I felt so mean and horrible.

"Jess, are you still there?" she'd said.

"Yes. Look, you know the signal is bad in Sarah's bedroom. I'd better go. Her parents are OK with me staying this weekend. It's for the best Mum, all right?"

"Well, I suppose so, but I want you home by lunch on Sunday and then we're going to have a few things out young lady."

In your dreams, I thought, I'll probably be in Rwanda by then. But I just said yes in a quiet voice and clicked off.

The climber's hut is mad. All those blokes snoring in one room. I hardly slept at all. Ryan dropped off straight away. It was so nice being close to him, hearing him breathe all night. I've never slept next to a boy before.

119

Sar and Max look so happy this morning. Not a care in the world. They're walking up ahead on the path hand-in-hand. She's carrying one of the bags with the climbing stuff in it and they're laughing and chatting away. Just like me and Ryan should be doing, only we're not. I'm walking a bit behind him and James is behind me, lugging a huge canvas sack.

James won't let me carry anything. "You've been ill," he said with a lovely smile just like Ryan's.

Ryan growled something at him; I didn't quite catch it. I think they're really close and that's why Ryan pretends James is a pain.

Not like me and Veeve. We've never been close.

The only one I was close to in my family was Dad.

And Nana Hat of course. What would *she* think if she saw me breaking plates in Mum's kitchen? "Mother never let us waste a crumb," she always says, and that's how she brought Dad up too. It seems to have had the opposite effect on him, spending money on us like it was water. Now all his money's gone and he's turned on me as if it's all *my* fault.

I can feel tears coming into my eyes again and I brush them away with the back of my hand. I glance ahead at Ryan but he's got his head down.

I think about all those texts yesterday. Was it another girl? But Ryan doesn't seem the type to cheat. Maybe they were from his Mum, checking he's taking care of James. That's quite sweet, really.

"We'll start with a bit of bouldering." Max's voice breaks

into my thoughts. He and Sarah have stopped in front of a big rock standing on its own away from the main cliff.

"I'm not going up that thing," I say to Sar and she gives me a grim nod. Now we're actually out here I think she's beginning to have second thoughts. She's taller than me by a few centimetres, but her arms are really thin. We both hate sports, and I'm so weak after being ill.

"It's easy, trust me," says Max and he unravels a mat and drops it on the ground. "Crash mat. In case you fall."

I catch James's eye and we exchange raised eyebrows.

Ryan has sloped off. I can see he's got his mobile in his hand, so I find a corner out of the wind and settle down on the ground, wrapping James's scarf closer round my neck.

Max and Sarah are totally absorbed in one another. He seems to be staring into her eyes as he puts a helmet on her head and spends ages doing up the chin strap.

James drops down close beside me and I feel a rush of warmth from his body.

"Smoke?" he says, offering me a cigarette.

Might warm me up, I think and I take one. We light up and he pulls out a can of Red Bull from his pocket.

"You going to have a go?" says James.

"Not sure. What about you?"

"Course," he says. "It's easy. Ryan won't. He's such a wuss. He'll never go up."

"But you two, you're really close aren't you? My sister's so jealous of me all the time."

James gives me a concerned look. I think he fancies me.

"Is that why you were out in the rain last night?" That's so sweet, he's worried about me.

"You don't know the half of it," I say and take a deep drag on the cigarette. I might as well get cancer and claim my old bed on the cancer ward. No more nonsense about rare illnesses and endless tests with no answers. The doctors will tell me it's lung cancer, self-inflicted, like not wearing your seatbelt, then put me on chemo until my hair falls out and Mum and the girls have to take me shopping for a wig – they'd love that.

"Jess?" James is staring at me. He must have said something.

"Sorry, honey, what?" I say. It makes me feel very grown up, calling him honey.

His face softens. He's got a nice face with a square jaw and dark hair, cut quite short, but not curly like Ryan's. He looks older than fourteen now, and he has very broad shoulders.

He puts his arm around me and I snuggle down a bit. He's only Ryan's little brother. I'm just beginning to feel warm for the first time today when a voice snarls, "What's going on?"

It's Ryan and he's standing over us, glaring at James as if he wants to turn him to stone.

James says, "Keeping your girlfriend warm for you."

Ryan looks as if he's going to punch James. James is only a kid, he can't be jealous, can he?

"Hey," I say, "we're just chilling." I wriggle away from James but Ryan's face is like thunder. "Ryan? What's the matter?"

He's clutching his phone and it bleeps again, like in the car yesterday, as though he's getting multiple messages at once.

"Who *is* that?" I ask, trying not to sound suspicious.

Ryan looks down at his phone. "Just Mum, she's a real worrier," he mutters. James splutters next to me, choking on his Red Bull. "You know you're not allowed that stuff!" Ryan yells.

"Drop dead," says James, and I must admit I'm a bit surprised. Maybe I got it wrong about these two, they don't sound any different to me and Veeve.

"Go and help Max," snaps Ryan.

"Make me," says James. He jumps to his feet, squaring up to Ryan, although he only comes up to his chin.

Suddenly I can see the blockhead in James.

Ryan gives James a little shove. "Just take that bag to Max," he says.

James puts the can down slowly on a rock and then swaggers off down the path, swinging the bag arrogantly.

So James isn't so nice after all. He needs a good slap, like my sister.

"Coming?" says Ryan, and I can't read the look on his face. He's closed down again like when he met me in the van last Sunday. Whatever's going on between those two, it seems serious. And suddenly it's like a light bulb going on in my head. All those texts, the mood switches, nearly getting into a fight with James.

Ryan has a problem too. Something's happened in the past week and he doesn't want me to know. So now we've both got a secret. Who's going to break down first and tell?

Chapter 19

Ryan

James is hitting on my girlfriend. I turn my back and he's all over her – and she looks like she's enjoying it. She can't prefer that little jerk to me. I shouldn't have kicked off, though, because now I'm sure she's guessed something's wrong. She keeps giving me suspicious looks.

Lee won't stop texting and calling me. I feel like smashing my phone against a rock. What does she expect me to do, all the way out here?

"Earth to Ryan." It's Max and he's standing by a huge rock. "We're doing this one first," he says and he hands me a helmet.

"Where's the rope?"

"Don't need it, trust me. It's a really easy climb, only about three metres; you could jump from the top."

But it looks so steep and I can't see any proper footholds. What if I got dizzy and fell? James would laugh his head off. And Jess? I don't know about Jess. We're not very close. Sarah and Max seem closer than us and they've been going out for less time.

"I'll go up first," says Max. "Show you where the holds are."

He turns to face the rock. He's changed into his climbing shoes, the expensive ones he showed me last week.

"Climbing's like problem solving," he's always telling me.

"You've got to think through your next move, next hold. But it's also about going for it."

I don't know how much I want to go for it.

He scans the boulder and then he reaches up to a bit of rock sticking out, which I hadn't even noticed, gets a firm grip with his left hand, does the same with his right hand a bit lower and then his left foot finds a crack and he's off the ground. Climbing slowly, testing each crack, he's up the boulder in a minute. He sits down, legs dangling and calls, "Watch me as I come down. James?"

James is texting, his head bent over his phone.

"You watching, James?" calls Max, and I feel the anger rise up in me again.

"Yeah, yeah," says James, not looking up.

Max climbs back down and then he says, "Who's next?"

I should volunteer really, but I'm scared of looking an idiot.

Then Sarah says, "I'll have a go."

I hear James snigger. But I don't want to be the first one up so I say, "Ladies first," and step back towards Jess.

She says, "Hey," quietly, and I put my arm around her.

She snuggles up and I start to calm down. It's so dumb to get mad at James, he's not worth it. It's Jessica Fitzgerald who matters, and whatever happens with Lee, me and Jess are out here together and she wants me, doesn't she?

Sarah starts to climb, putting her foot on the same place as Max, but when she reaches for the handholds she slips and falls back with a frightened scream. I feel the sweat prickle in my armpits.

Max catches her under her shoulders. "Try again," he says, "you can do it."

Sarah looks round at Jess who gives her the thumbs up, so she turns back, wipes her palms down her jeans and goes for the handholds first this time. Then, with a sort of grunt, she lifts her foot onto the rock and pushes up. As she leaves the ground everyone cheers.

"Watch your feet," calls out Max in a calm voice. "Push up, don't pull up from your hands."

She goes a bit further and then she stops. "I can't, Max, there isn't a foothold. I want to come down."

"There's a nice bit of rock to your left, see it?"

"No, I can't, where?" her voice is really wobbly.

"That's it, bit further, your foot's nearly there. Yes! You've got it."

Sarah lets out a whoop and she's more than halfway up. Two more pushes and she's clinging to the top, yelling, "I did it, look at me, look at me!"

Everyone cheers again and some climbers on the main rock face cheer back.

Jess gives me a squeeze and as we kiss James gives a mocking laugh. Who cares, I think, tightening my arms around Jess. His girlfriend's miles away, so I score today.

Sarah climbs back down and jumps or slips off the last metre or so, but Max is ready and catches her. She and Jess jump up and down screaming at each other and Max goes a bit red.

"You going up now, mate?" he asks me.

"Yes, go on Ryan," says Jess and she bumps shoulders with me.

I lick my lips, which have gone strangely dry. James is the sporty one; I just get under my van and muck about with tools. I never saw myself as a rock climber. But I can't chicken out now.

I turn to face the rock, tighten the strap on my helmet and reach up. My palms are so sweaty I'm sure they're going to slip, but I find the holds and grip as hard as I can. I'm almost too scared to lift my foot.

"Just by your left knee," says Max. "Put your foot on it, that's right, now push up."

My knee is actually shaking, but I push and suddenly I'm off the ground and there's the rock looming up above me.

"That's it mate, you're doing fine. Got the right foot too, great. Now reach the right hand up to that crack, straight up, you've got it, and the left. No, don't look up, look down at your feet, push, move your feet up. Yes, that's it. Now, Ryan, go on!"

I think I've frozen on the rock with terror and I'll never move, or I'll just fall backwards onto the crash mat and break my neck or something.

But then I hear James say, "You wuss, Ryan, should have been at the top by now!"

That does it. I'm really angry and I shove my foot right up onto a really high bit of rock sticking out. I push down hard and I'm at the top.

I can't believe it. It's fantastic. I'm standing right on top of the boulder, miles above everyone else, feeling like I just climbed Everest. Max lets out a piercing whistle between his teeth.

"You're a natural, mate," he calls up to me.

I feel all puffed up. Max says I'm a natural climber and I never even knew.

I'm back down on the ground in three or four moves. Jess flings her arms round my neck and we lock in a long warm kiss. That makes all the fear worth it.

"Your turn now, James," says Max.

"Later," says James. "I'll do it when we get to the more interesting stuff."

Max takes us along the path to a different boulder. "This one gives you a chance to traverse a little bit. I'll show you what I mean."

He goes up about a metre and then moves to the left another metre. "You can smear at this point if you want," he says and flattens the top half of his foot against the rock. "If that doesn't feel secure, there's a foothold just below." He moves his foot down to a crack wide enough for a good toehold. Then he's at the top and climbs back down.

"This is a good way to try out a traverse, a sideways move, before we do Monks Pedestal," he says.

All the climbs have names. Some of them are really crazy, like Late Night Final, Chip Shop Brawl and Torture Garden. Max told me about them – he reads them up in the climbers' guidebook. And then there's the climbers' code, etiquette Max calls it. "The climbing world is a bit old-fashioned," he told me. "Polite and respectful."

Max is trained to lead climbing. That means he has to set the route and put the nuts in to pull the rope through for the next climber. And he has to be totally reliant on himself. He loves it, but it's dangerous stuff. If you fall before you get the first nut in, there's nothing to stop you crashing down all the way.

"I fell once when I was leading in Scotland," Max told me once. "The rope stretched, I flipped upside down and my head stopped about seven centimetres from the ground. But the nut held."

"Christ!" I said.

Max grinned. "Everyone falls. I was lucky. You get up and do it again. It's in my blood."

It's a climber's dream to be the first to find a new route and give it a name.

"Experienced climbers are careful who they share their knowledge with, you don't want a novice thinking they can try something they're not ready for," Max said.

So Max has secrets too, only they're good secrets. What will he say when I tell him my secret?

James decides to try a boulder called Flips Nightmare. He starts too quickly, showing off of course, and falls straight back down. "Ouch," he yells.

"OK?" asks Max, and James nods, rubbing his knee. He's just making a fuss, wants to be the centre of attention as usual.

He starts again and then he's up to the traverse. I don't fancy that move at all, it looks really awkward.

Max calls up, "That's it, mate, doing well, now stretch your left foot sideways onto that hold, see it?"

James is clinging to the rock and he turns his head, lets go for a second and almost falls backwards again. My heart leaps into my mouth. Mum'll kill me! But he scrabbles back onto the holds and leans his head against the rock, panting hard.

"Well done, mate. Don't worry, I'm here," calls up Max, and I'm sure there's a slight wobble in his voice. Does he really know what he's doing? Then he goes on calmly, "Rest for a minute, get your breath back and then try again. Try for that foothold to your left."

"I can't reach it. My legs are shorter than yours, Max. Aren't they, Ryan?" I feel this little pull inside me as he says my name. He's only a kid, I remind myself. But I can see the hold and he *can* do it.

So I call out, "You're fine, your legs are long enough."

That seems to fire him up. He stretches his foot out, finds the hold and then he's across with a whoop. The last bit's easy and he's at the top, dangling his legs and yelling down at us, "It's easy, come on you loser!"

I give it a go and the traverse is just as bad as I thought it would be, but somehow I make it and I feel great when I'm on the top.

Then Jess decides to have a go.

"Are you sure?" I ask.

"No. But Sarah doesn't want to be the only girl."

I stand next to Max to watch her go up. But she only gets as far as getting her feet off the ground before she stops, clinging to the rock.

"Everything's shaking, Max," she says and her voice is close to tears. "I can't do it, my muscles are like jelly."

"Rest a minute."

But Jess has her face pressed to the rock and she doesn't look too good.

"I'll fall, I will. Sar, I'll fall," she cries out, panicking.

"Jess, babes, we're right here," calls out Sarah. "Come on, Max, let her down, she can't do it."

Max nods. "OK, climb down here, I'll catch you if you slip." Jess sort of slides down the rock and lands with a cry in Max's arms.

"My knees are all scraped," she says and pulls up her jeans.

Both knees are bleeding. I feel terrible, we should never have let her go up. She's not well enough.

"Time for some first aid," says Max breezily. "Got those sandwiches, Sarah?"

The students made a stack of sandwiches this morning and Sarah charmed them into giving us some. She pulls the bulging plastic bags from her pack, lays down Max's jacket on a flat rock and sets out the food. I realise I'm starving.

Max gets his first aid box out and cleans Jess's knees, and he also checks the cut on her hand. "How did you do this?" he asks.

I catch her eye and she gives me a quick frown. Then she says, "I broke a glass. Cut my hand picking the pieces up."

"Must have been a great party?" says James with a matey grin. What a dumb thing to say. Jess gives him a wary look. Maybe she's finally getting the message about my blockhead brother.

Is she telling the truth? That cut might well be from a bit of broken glass, but maybe her Dad threw the glass at her. I wish she'd tell me what's going on.

But then maybe that would mean I have to tell her about Lee and the baby.

God.

Chapter 20
Jess

I'm *never* doing that again. I thought I was going to be killed. I couldn't find anywhere proper for my hands. It was the most scared I've been since hospital. No, since I saw Dad take the money from the wallets. That picture still goes round and round in my head. I thought it might fade away out here. No such luck.

"Another sandwich?" It's Ryan.

I shake my head.

"Do you want to go back to the hut? I'll come with you?"

He's so nice, my boyfriend, isn't he? Whatever's worrying him, I'm sure he'll tell me soon enough and he'll understand everything when we leave for Africa. I'm going to tell him the whole story once we've crossed the Channel and I'm away from my so-called family.

"I'm OK."

Ryan takes off his hoody and hands it to me. I snuggle into it and pull the hood over my ears. "What about you?" He's got just a thin, long-sleeved polo shirt on now.

"You get really warm climbing. You going to have another go?"

"What do you think I am, a blockhead?"

Ryan and me exchange looks and burst into laughter.

Sar looks up questioningly, but neither of us explain.

"Private joke," says Sar, but she's grinning and I can see she's happy I've cheered up.

We pack up and Max takes us along the path to another climb. Ryan puts his arm round me and James lags behind, talking on his mobile.

We pass the students, who are already climbing on some high rock walls. Max calls out, "Toby, are you soloing Elegy today?"

"If the weather holds," says Toby, adjusting the rope on his harness. Then he shouts, "Climbing," to the guy on the ground paying out the rope.

"Toby's jamming," says Max. "Watch his technique, he's very experienced."

Toby's climbing up a single narrow crack, jamming his hands and then his feet into the gap in the rock. It's really hard work, hand over foot, pushing himself upwards.

Then he stops and hangs on the rock with one hand, peering all around. I feel giddy just staring up at him.

"He's at the crux," says Max quietly. "That's the most tricky part of a climb. He just has to go for it."

Everyone is quiet for a bit, exchanging looks, but no one seems impatient.

Then someone yells out, "Go on, Tobes!"

Toby raises his left foot so high his knee is almost in his neck, and then with a sudden move he's up and onto a small ledge. My knees feel weak but everyone's nodding and the same voice calls out, "Bit reachy, mate."

"Tell me about it," calls down Toby with a grin on his face.

As we walk on James calls ahead to us, "Dare you to do that."

"Don't be stupid!" snaps Max.

I give Ryan's arm a squeeze and we lock eyes. We don't even need to say blockhead. We just know. We walk on until the students are out of sight. I warm up a bit but once we stop I can feel that it's getting much colder.

"Not many people come up here in November," says Max. "That's how I like it best."

We're standing at the base of a rock wall and Max starts handing out harnesses to everyone except me. "Sit this one out, Jess?" he says and I nod. "James, do something useful."

"Like what?" says James in a bored voice, his eyes still glued to his mobile.

"Get some wood together for a fire," says Ryan. "Jess needs to warm up."

James looks like he's going to argue and then he looks over at me shivering away, and he nods and wanders off.

Sarah and Max start rooting around in the bags for all the equipment and Ryan comes over and puts his arms round me. I huddle down and he says, "Sorry."

"That's my line."

"Yeah, but I didn't want you to get so cold – can't have you getting sick again, even though you wanted to come on this trip because of ... well, your Dad, or whatever."

"Mmm," I say, playing for time. Shall I tell him the truth about Dad? It feels so good being here in his arms, so warm and safe. But what if I tell him and he doesn't get it? What if he thinks I have a terrible family, criminals and all that? I've met his family and I don't think they'd ever steal anything, even James, he's just a pain, not a thief. If Ryan turned against me I couldn't stand it right now.

So I say, "Let's make a promise."

"What sort of promise?"

"When we leave for Africa we won't talk about blockhead stuff, ever again."

"O-k-a-y," he says slowly. "Er, about Africa—" He stops.

My heart does a double back flip. Well done, Jess, I think, you've stuffed that up.

"You know when I rang you on Friday? When you were stuck out in the rain and all that?" he says in a bit of a rush. "Well, I was going to ask you, you know, just so I didn't get things wrong or anything. I mean, what about your parents, will they let you, and also...." Also? I think. Does he have another girlfriend? All those texts. "Er, do you have a passport?" he finishes.

I laugh out loud with relief and it comes out almost as a scream. "Is that what you were worried about?" I ask him and he nods.

Yay!! I've got the sweetest, the best, the most gorgeous boyfriend in the world. Paige Slapper Butcher is welcome to Scott.

Me and Ryan, we're off to Africa!

Chapter 21

Ryan

Monk's Pedestal. In the guidebook they call it Severe. That's two levels above the last climb. Very different and much harder. It's mid-afternoon. It'll be dark in an hour but Max has been looking forward to the Pedestal all day.

"We're not doing it, right, Sar?" says Jess. She gives a little shiver and stretches out her hands towards the fire.

"Come on, Sarah," says Max.

"You are joking me, aren't you?" says Sarah. "I'm not breaking any more nails."

Max's face falls. He catches my eye and I give him the thumbs up. I can't let him down now.

He starts to explain the climb. "I'm going to climb up and set the anchor at the top. On the way I'll put in all the nuts." He holds up a stiff wire looped through a wedge-shaped piece of metal at one end. "This is the nut and this…." he holds up another piece, "is a krab. You need those to clip on to a runner or a fixed point on the rock."

I remember the karabiner, or krab as the climbers call them, from his Dad's shop. They have a snap-link and you have to be able to open them with one hand, while you grip the rock with the other. But we haven't had much practice.

"OK," says Sarah with a grin, "so you grab a nut and ram it in the crack, clip on a krab and smear all the way to the top…."

" ... applying lip gloss halfway up," finishes Jess and the girls collapse giggling.

Max ignores them and says, "Watch as I climb up so you see where the holds are."

"Who's holding your rope?" asks James.

"I'm the leader, mate, so I take the rope up and Ryan's the belayer, paying out the rope for me."

"Oh, superhero stuff," says James.

"Show some respect," I snarl.

The weather's getting much colder and Jess is looking pale and shivery. The sky's gone a sort of white-grey and it won't be light for much longer.

"We'll make this the last climb, mate," I say in a low voice to Max. "Jess doesn't look good."

He glances over to the girls, who are huddled together on the ground, and nods.

"Just you and James on this one, then. James first and then Ryan, you finish as you'll need to collect the nuts and that's hard."

Max is adjusting the rack of equipment round his waist. If he falls ... but I don't think about that. He's been leading climbs for years in his club. He's preparing for Everest. He can do a Severe with one hand tied behind his back.

Then James says, "*I* want to go third."

"You'll have to collect all the nuts, pull them out the cracks with one hand and bring them up to me," says Max. "Think you can do all that without slipping?"

"Yeah, course I can," says James. "Anyway, so what if I leave one behind."

Max rounds on him, "Each nut costs at least ten pounds, that's what, so there won't be much left from your pocket money, will there?"

"All right, keep your hair on, I'll bring all the stuff up," sneers James.

Max glances at me. I don't want a scene and I want Jess back in the warm as soon as possible. I nod and say, "If you think he's ready."

Max takes off. The first bit's straightforward. Then he stops at the traverse. Above his head is a roof, a wide overhang. That's why we have to move across the rock to a little ledge sticking out and then go round the overhang. Max starts across, wedging nuts at metre intervals as he goes, clipping the rope through and checking it runs smoothly. He gets to the ledge and sits on it for a minute to rest. It's about fifteen metres above the ground. Way too high to jump down. Once you get that far you're committed. No turning back. The final stage is to climb round the side of the overhang until you reach the top of the climb.

Max reaches the top and sends the rope down.

Jess gets up and comes over to me. "Just checking your knot," she says, pulling on the rope where it's looped through my harness.

It feels quite sexy and I blush as she kisses my cheek. She smells so sweet and fresh. I'm all sweaty after a morning of climbing but she doesn't seem to notice.

"Break a leg," says James with a sneer on his face.

I ignore him and call to Max, "Climbing." I feel the tension as he pulls in the rope.

The beginning of the climb is tricky. My fingers hurt as they try to get a hold on the tiny cracks and get up to a better foothold. I'm panting like mad and my palms are slippery with sweat.

"All right?" Max calls down. His voice feels as though it's floating disembodied in the freezing air. "Mate?"

"Yeah, just resting," I say and I lean my face against the rock. The light seems to be getting dimmer and I can't see very far across the downs. All I want is a beer and to feel my feet firmly on the ground.

Let's get this over with, I tell myself, and I unclip the next nut. Fear floods my body. I'm fumbling with the krab, my fingers slipping, but I manage to move the knot and clip back on. There're two more nuts before I even get to the traverse.

Somehow I move upwards and then I'm at the traverse. I feel the prickle in my armpits.

"On the traverse," I call out. It's a bit more of a stretch and then I reach for a handhold and miss. I tip backwards for half a second and grab for the rock, screaming out. Christ! My stomach clenches as I look down. Too far to jump. The only way is up. I lean my face against the rock and breathe in.

"Doing really well, mate."

Max's voice calms me. I wipe my hands one at a time on my jeans and set off across the rock. James had better not mess this up, I think, as I move past the nuts. He should have gone up first.

I move on and then lean back, relaxing for a few seconds before I pass another nut. It's a bit easier this time – I'm getting used to it. James'll be OK. I haul myself onto the ledge and sit there with my legs swinging over.

"Ready when you are," calls Max.

"Climbing," I say, and the last ten metres are really easy. I swing over the top and Max is banging me on the back and laughing. It's even colder up here and the visibility is getting worse. My hands freeze really quickly as the sweat dries and I tuck them under my arms.

"OK, you go back down over there," says Max, "but be careful, it's a hard scramble. Don't want any broken ankles."

The route down is quite awkward. The rocks are large and difficult to get over. I nearly fall forward at one point and crack my elbow as I reach out to stop myself.

"That was brilliant!" Jess is running up to me laughing and she grabs me round the neck. "You looked so cool."

I shrug modestly but secretly I'm glowing. It feels like it's a pretty big thing I've done, almost like taking on Africa, and Jess seeing me is, well, awesome.

"You going?" I say to James, who's still sprawled on the ground in front of the fire.

"Might as well." He acts like he's not bothered but he gets up and puts on his helmet. Then he starts to reach up the rock.

"You're supposed to say 'Climbing'" I snap.

"Climb-ing," James calls out in a mocking voice. He grins over his shoulder at the girls, and Sarah laughs.

"Get on with it, you jerk."

James inches slowly up the rock and gets to the first nut.

"What do I do now?" he yells to Max.

"Pull the nut out and clip it on your harness."

James is leaning back a bit too far as he tugs on the nut and I'm about to yell at him when the nut comes away and he sways to one side.

"Whoa!" he shouts, his voice ending in a squeak.

"OK, mate," calls down Max. "Well done, come on to the next one."

James raises his foot to a hold and pushes up until he's at the next nut. But that one doesn't seem to want to come out. He tugs and tugs with one hand, almost losing his grip on the rock with the other. I can hear him cursing away.

"It's stuck ... stupid ... ow!"

"What's up?" says Max.

"Pinched my finger," moans James. "I can't get it out, it'll just have to stay there."

"Come on mate, do me a favour, that's the expensive one." Max sounds really annoyed.

"You come and get it then, I'm going on."

James moves on until he reaches the traverse. He stops and I think he's going to chicken out. Part of me hopes he does.

Then he says, "Ready," and starts across the traverse. He's not so sure here and his foot slips a couple of times. He rests his face against the rock for a second before moving on to the next nut. He starts to tug on it really hard this time.

"Make sure you get this one," calls out Max. "You on a good foothold?"

Max can't see him and now that the light is fading so fast, it's difficult for me to see clearly, too.

"I think so," says James.

I feel my stomach clench again. There's a strong, sharp smell of danger in the air. It'll be OK, I tell myself. He'll do it and then we can all go home.

I squint back up at James. He sort of lunges, wrenching hard, and suddenly the nut comes out and he slips or misses, or I don't know what, but his body is coming away from the rock. It's falling and in a split second he's flipped upside down, swinging left in a pendulum and his face crashes into the rock. There is the most awful sound, like the high-pitched scream of a wounded dog. I feel my lunch coming up my throat.

"James! Max! God, he's fallen."

"I've got him, I've got him!" Max yells. "James, reach your arms out, see the ledge, grab it mate."

"Ryan!" James shrieks in a voice that chills me to the bone. I'm reaching up the rock to try and grab his head but he's way out of reach. Can I climb up to him without a rope? Oh God! The rock is scraping the skin off my fingers and my muscles are straining and stretching until I'm in agony.

"Hang on!" I roar back. "Max won't let you go." He'd better not or I'll kill him.

We're all yelling instructions and James is screaming and the girls scream back. Then, somehow, he manages to turn back upright.

He'll be OK, he'll be OK, runs feverishly through my

head. He's got to be. What's Mum going to say?!

James manages to grab the rock and get a handhold and then his hand slips off again. His arms are waving about in a sort of swimming movement and he looks as though he's drowning in midair. But somehow he gets his hands and feet on the rock and then, sobbing and cursing, he reaches up to the ledge and hauls himself to safety.

The girls cheer and clap and jump up and down.

"James, sweetie, hang on, you're safe," Sarah yells up.

I'm so relieved I'm almost crying.

That was the worst moment of my entire life.

James is sobbing, his whole body curled up on the ledge against the rock wall, his head in his hands.

Max calls out in a shaky voice, "He's OK, Ryan, he's on the ledge. It'll be OK now, I promise, I'll get him down."

"He nearly crashed to the bottom. He could have been killed!" I yell up in a real fury now.

"Mate, God, I'm so sorry, but he was never going all the way. My anchor's bombproof, trust me. We just got to lower him down."

I can see Max standing upright, peering over the edge.

"Do it," I say. "Get him down, now."

James hasn't moved and I'm half-expecting Max to climb down and carry him back to us.

Jess comes over and puts her arm through mine. "What about those students?" she says.

"Haven't seen them for ages," I mutter.

"Want me to go and look for them?" says Sarah and I shoot her a grateful smile.

But James is calling to me, "Ryan, come and get me, I can't hang on, I'm scared, come and get me," and I swear it's breaking my heart.

At the end of the day he's my blood, as the gangs say; he's my little brother and he needs me. Maybe he mucked up my life, but right now I just want him down and safe.

"Max, what's the plan?" I yell up.

"I'm thinking, I'm thinking!" Max hollers back, but his voice is all over the place. Like he's lost control or something.

"Get on with it!"

"All right, OK, James, listen. This is what you gotta do. Sit up on the ledge and let your legs dangle over the edge. Then when you're ready, just turn round and push off and I'll lower you down. You'll be fine, honest, trust me. I've done this loads of times."

But James doesn't move. His hands are gripping the rock now and the rope has gone slack. Max can't lower him like that.

"James, do what Max says," I call up. "I'll catch you at the bottom, I won't let you drop, I...."

But James cuts me off and his voice is so pitiful, "I can't, Ryan, I'm scared."

"Poor kid," murmurs Jess in my ear.

"What's the number for mountain rescue?" says Sarah, and she's got her phone out.

"No idea," I say, "and anyway, there's no time, is there? He's terrified."

"Ryan, don't leave me here." James's voice is getting quieter. What if he passes out?

"Max, you've got to get him down. Now!" No answer. Max the great mountain climber has lost it. "I'm coming up, we've got to sort it!"

"No, look, mate, it's a really tough scramble. You could break something."

Yeah, your skull if we don't get my brother back down very soon, I think grimly.

I feel a hand on my shoulder. It's Jess. "Be careful, Ryan," she says in a low voice and kisses my cheek.

Sarah's laying out the crash mat, as if that'll be any use in a fifteen metre fall.

I start up the rocks at the side, the way I came down, back up to Max. James is still silent. The sky has gone completely white and it feels a tiny bit warmer. Then it begins to snow. I don't believe it!

Great big white flakes, without any warning, pouring out of the sky, landing on my face and hands and sticking like icing to the rock.

"Crissakes!" Max's voice floats down to me through the swirling snowflakes. He lets out a string of swear words. "Mate, you gotta go dead careful now."

My feet skid off the side of a rock and my ankle twists sharply as my foot gets caught. My fingers are frozen as the snow settles on them, and they slip straight off the rock. The sweat trickles down my back. Fear is beginning to balloon inside my stomach. Then my left foot shoots off completely and I nearly drop backwards.

There's a couple of smothered screams from below and

Max calls out in a frightened voice, "What?"

I'm struggling to get my foothold and I hear Jess call up, "He's OK, you're OK, Ryan."

I'm shaking with fear and cold. The snow is getting heavier and heavier. Max is crazy to bring us up here in winter. He thinks he's such an expert. Why did I trust him? He's such a big mouth, always going on about his stupid climbing. But I make myself stop. I can't concentrate *and* be angry at Max. I remember what he told me, "Climbing is like problem solving."

So this is my problem: the rocks are white with snow, my hands and feet are freezing and I've nearly fallen once. OK, stop! I yell inside my head. Think about the next move. Left hand. Good, now your left foot. Great. Right hand, right foot. One move at a time. Almost there, haul your body, Ryan, push up from your legs. Done it!

Max, his beanie hat white with snow, looms up through the storm. I look out across the downs and all I can see is swirling snow.

"You made it mate, awesome."

"Yeah, yeah, ok, what's the plan?"

"Plan? Apart from making him stand up so I can lower him down?"

"We can't *make* him."

Max stares wildly around him and then he says. "Only one thing for it. Abseil down to him."

"Why didn't you say so before! Get on with it!" I yell at him.

But he shakes his head. "Not me mate, you. I have to stay

here on the rope to lower both of you down."

"Me? But I've never done *anything* like that!"

"You'll have to, there's no other way. You abseil down, clip yourselves together and I'll lower you both to the ground."

I can't believe this. He'll get us both killed.

"Look mate," Max says, "I know it's not ideal but trust me, it'll work. I'll change the anchor onto that huge rock."

He stops and there's a silence. The temperature seems to be dropping again and I'm feeling much colder. James must be frozen.

"Let's do it," I say grimly.

Max talks me through the abseil. "You keep the rope at your side and let yourself down a bit at a time. Keep a firm grip on the rope or it'll run through your hand and burn you," he says, clipping me on. "You got to lean right back, Ryan, and walk down the rock. You OK with this?"

"Do I have much choice?" I say, grimly.

I turn my back to the edge and I'm almost paralysed with fear. I can't see anything below me and the snow is settling on my eyelashes, half blinding me. I can hardly bear the thought of leaning out over the edge. It feels suicidal. For a minute I think of refusing.

Then James calls out: "Where are you, Ryan?"

"I'm coming," I call down, but it comes out as a nervous croak.

I take a deep breath, lean right back against the rope and start down. My feet are slipping all the time on the icy rock and then my hand loses its grip. Before I can tighten it again, the rope runs through my hand and burns the palm of my hand.

I scream out and Max yells, "Mate?"

"Rope burn," I yell back.

"Go more slowly," he calls.

It's such a struggle; the snow is swirling around me and I'm so cold. Jess must be frozen too. We should never have come. My life seems to be one long regret at the moment. I should never have gone with Lee. I should never have let James go last.

How much further to the ledge? I can't see anything and I'm scared to look down in case I swing out.

"Ryan!"

I'm there and James is grabbing my legs and then I'm on the ledge. James throws his arms around me. He's sobbing, and I'm shaking and sweating and shivering. But I did it!

"What now, Max?" I yell out.

"Clip your harness to James. Stand up and I'll take in the slack. When you're ready, call out 'Climbing' and step off the edge, same as you did up here. I'll lower you down."

I unclip the link. My hands are so numb I can hardly snap the gate open. James just clings on to me. It takes two or three goes and then we're clipped together.

"James, listen!" I shout above the wind. "We're going to stand up now and you'll feel Max take in the rope."

He doesn't move and I think he's going to refuse. Then he starts to get up. I wait until he's upright, his hands clinging on to the rock. Then I stand and call, "Climbing."

I'm afraid James won't step off at the last minute and I'll have to prise his fingers off the rock. I put my hands round his waist and gently ease him backwards. I feel his hands tense the grip on the rock and the sweat pricks my armpits again. Come on, mate, I think. Just do it.

Then his arms fall by his side, his feet start to shuffle and I step into nothing, pulling him with me. For a split second it feels as if we're falling. Max has got it wrong again, oh God!

Then the rope tightens and I'm walking us down the rock face. The girls are calling out encouragement all the way and finally my feet are back on solid earth. We tumble to the ground and snow covers my eyelids.

Someone unclips the link and James rolls away. I reach up my hand to wipe my eyes and someone grabs it.

"You're a hero," says Jess with a giggle.

Then she's lying full on top of me, kissing the snow away and when I open my eyes I am looking straight into hers. I put my arms around her; we have never held each other so close and for so long.

But this is no good. We can't do this.

No way am I going to get another girl pregnant. I roll her off my body. Her eyes widen with hurt and amazement.

She doesn't get it, how could she?

Chapter 22

Jess

My jeans are soaked! Ryan didn't even find it romantic when I jumped on top of him and kissed him. He just pushed me right over into the snow. What is the *matter* with him?

Sar didn't notice. She's busy with the first aid kit.

Then Max comes back, calling out, "Is he OK? Anything broken? Mate, I'm *so* sorry."

Ryan's on his feet and he's bending over James, taking off his helmet. James's face is streaked with tears and blood but he's not unconscious or anything. Ryan's feeling all over his arms and legs and saying, "Does this hurt? Or this?"

"No," says James in a shaky voice.

"Ryan, mate, you're a legend," says Max, but Ryan just ignores him. Max turns to Sarah and says, "Pass me the kit, I'll sort him out."

But Ryan snatches it away and turns back to James. Sarah gives Max a hard look and then she goes off hunting about for something at the bottom of the rock face.

"Here we are, James," says Ryan in a really gentle voice. "I'll just clean you up."

He tears open an antiseptic wipe and starts dabbing at a long thin cut on James's face. There's a big hole in the knee of his jeans and he's lost one of his trainers on the way down.

They look as if they're in a little bubble all by themselves as the snow falls, settling on their hair and their shoulders. They don't need the rest of us, they're a unit, brothers sticking up for each other against the world.

No one in my family seems to care about me anymore. I thought Dad would ring me last night but I haven't had any calls or messages since Mum rang when we were in the car. Why hasn't Veeve texted me to see if I'm OK?

Last night, when I couldn't sleep, I kept thinking about Mum and Dad and Veeve sitting round in the living room, all cosy and warm, going on about how spoilt I am and how I'm always getting my own way, and how it serves me right going out in the rain. I mean, I know that wasn't true: Veeve came out looking for me and Dad cleared up the mess in the kitchen and Mum called. But still, they've just left me all alone this weekend – after I went insane in front of them. I wonder what they've told Nana Hat. What if they turn her against me too?

I feel my eyes fill up with tears and look round for Sarah, but she's hunting around at the bottom of the rocks.

"Here." Sarah's found the lost trainer and she reaches out for James's foot to put it back on. "Yuck," she says. "Your sock is soaked. Anyone got a spare pair?"

"Yes," Max says and rushes over to his pack. He scrabbles about like mad, finds the socks and runs back to Sarah like an excited puppy trying to please.

"Dry socks won't mend a broken head," growls Ryan.

Max's head drops and he turns away. That's a bit harsh, I think, but Ryan's so focused on James I don't dare speak up.

Then James says, "Don't tell Mum," in such a little voice me and Sar can't help laughing.

"You're so sweet, a brave little man," says Sarah, and even Ryan is smiling a bit.

"I was rubbish," says James, his eyes fixed on Ryan. "My big brother saved my life."

Ryan mutters about it being nothing.

"That wasn't nothing, mate. It was heroic," says Max.

"I didn't have any choice, you idiot!" Ryan turns on Max and gives him a hard push. Max almost loses his balance and his expression is hurt and surprise all at once. "What were you thinking, making him do all that? He's only a little kid, you could have killed him!"

"Whoa, mate, take it easy," says Max. His voice is a bit unsteady and he looks like he might push Ryan back. "It was an accident, I'm sorry. I'd never do anything to hurt you or your brother, you know that Ryan, we're best mates."

"You took a stupid risk, you're always boasting about everything you know about climbing." Ryan's face is furious and he's really shouting now. "Admit it, you don't know *anything!*"

Ryan's fists are bunched up and Max has taken a step backwards. God! If they have a fight now, we'll never get back. We'll die of cold out here tonight.

Sarah looks at me and I shrug. "Come on, guys," she says quietly, "we've got to get James back to the hut."

Ryan is still all pumped up and he's glaring at Max who can hardly meet his eye. It doesn't matter how much of a blockhead James can be, he's Ryan's little brother and that's what matters to Ryan. Not like my pathetic family. No loyalty to blood there. They've already forgotten how ill I was, how we thought I was going to die. And Dad? Well, he doesn't seem to care about anybody but himself. Loyalty in my family? What a joke!

Max turns away first and mutters something about going back up to get the ropes and stuff. Ryan starts gathering all the equipment into the bags. Sarah helps him, and I sit next to James and try to keep him warm. Ryan keeps looking over at James, as if to check he's really there and all in one piece.

No one speaks. It feels so weird, as if we are suddenly a bunch of strangers. A bit like back home, when I felt like my family were about to tell me I was adopted.

Once all the stuff's packed up, we walk back in silence to the car. My hands and feet are so cold I can't feel them anymore. It takes ages to get the heater going. Max drives, hunched over the wheel, Sarah murmuring to him in the front seat. The windscreen wipers are on full, swishing the snowflakes back and forth.

Ryan leans towards me after a bit and whispers, "Max is such a blockhead. He could have killed James and all he cares about is getting his stupid equipment back home. I'll never trust him again."

Our eyes are locked together and we're staring and staring at each other. I feel as if I'm drinking him in, letting him pour through me like warm water. We're both wounded; we've both been let down. If we're going on this road trip together we have to have complete trust.

"I need to tell you something," I whisper.

"I know," he says.

What? I think in terror. He can't!

"It's your Dad, isn't it? He's been knocking you about."

I almost laugh out loud. Is that what he thinks? The truth is so much worse. I can't tell him everything, but I'm not going to lie to him anymore either. I'm going to tell him as much as I can.

I shake my head, "No, that's not it, although he did push me and my face hit the wall and he didn't do anything to stop me falling."

"I knew it!"

"But that's not really the problem. The cut on my hand, he didn't do that, although it happened because of him."

"So what is it? Tell me Jess, you can trust me."

I almost say that I will tell him, if he tells me his secret, but I don't because I just want to be honest for my own sake.

"All I can tell you is that there's a big problem with my Dad and I'm the only one that knows. I have to keep it secret from Mum and my big sister, Veeve. But we had the most terrible row and I ran out of the house on Friday night."

"What's the problem?"

I rub a hand across my eyes and then I say, "I can't tell you yet, but I will when I'm ready."

His head drops and I think he's angry with me. I don't blame him. But then he looks back up at me again and he says, "Don't worry, babe, it's going to be OK."

Babe! He never says anything like that.

"Hey," I say, and I cover his lips with my mouth. He doesn't push me away this time and we kiss until we run out of breath. Maybe we'll get through this. I need Ryan. There isn't anyone else, is there?

As we sink into each other's arms I can see the trees flash past, weighed down with snow, but beyond, everything is dark. We'll be back in the hut soon and I'll sleep next to Ryan again tonight and listen to him breathing. Then tomorrow we'll go home and make proper plans for Africa.

Everything's going to be OK. I know it.

Chapter 23

No one wakes up in the hut until nearly midday.

It takes ages to get ourselves going. Max insists on making everyone toast and eggs.

"Need something proper after yesterday," he says, grinning nervously around the kitchen area. Sarah's putting out plates but Ryan's glued to his mobile already. He's hardly spoken to me since we got up. And I don't think he's made it up with Max yet.

Last night we pushed our bunks right together. As we crawled exhausted into bed, Ryan whispered to me, "I don't trust Max anymore."

"It won't matter when we're on the road trip," I whispered back.

He didn't answer but he put his arms around me and we both fell asleep. I woke up all warm and cosy, my head on Ryan's chest. I lay there feeling the rise and fall of his breath as he slept.

I've decided to tell him the whole truth about Dad today. I'll do it in the car on the way home, once Max puts the music on. Then no one else will hear. I'll tell Ryan my secret and then he can tell me his and we'll start all over again with a clean sheet.

Everyone's fussing around James as they eat Max's breakfast. James looks really shattered. He had such a terrible scare yesterday. Ryan won't let him do anything, not even roll up his sleeping bag.

Finally all the food is eaten, the plates washed up and the car packed. Ryan takes James out and makes sure he's comfortable in the back, I climb into the middle row and Sarah and Max get in the front. It's gloomy outside but at least it isn't snowing.

Ryan starts texting almost immediately. I want to talk to him about Dad, but he's got to listen properly.

"Someone important?" I say and nod to the mobile.

Ryan looks up and then down again. He taps a couple of keys then turns off his phone. He checks over his shoulder. James is fast asleep. In the front Sar and Max are murmuring quietly to each other.

He turns to me and says, "I really, you know, *really,* like you, Jess."

"Me too," I say and I smile, but he doesn't smile back.

"I don't want to, you know, you've been so sick and what with your Dad, but...."

"It doesn't matter, not when I'm with you." He goes very quiet. "Ryan?" I say. Did I get this wrong? "Ryan?" He doesn't speak for ages and I think maybe he has fallen asleep.

Then he starts again and his voice is so full of sadness and fear. "The thing is, I, well, me and this girl...." Oh God! A chill goes right through me. "... she, well, her name's Lee and she lives with her Dad in Portsmouth, but that doesn't matter does it...." It *is* another girl! Just like Scott and Paige. "It was only one night at a beach party, September, ages before you and me, you know, before we became, an item?" He looks at me as if he thinks I'm going to deny

158

that we're an item, and laugh at him. We *are* an item. Why would I disagree?

He goes on, "Lee rang me last Sunday morning, before you and me went to the oyster beds. She said ... she said she's ... pregnant ... and it's mine."

It's like a punch in the stomach. Like when I saw Dad steal the money from the wallets. It's like – I don't know what it's like. All the air seems to go out of my lungs.

"I didn't tell you," Ryan is saying in a rapid voice, as if he doesn't want to give me a chance to say anything, "because Lee, well Lee and me, haven't even decided if she's going to keep it or not. But she keeps ringing and texting me, nagging me about coming over to tell her Dad. She can't keep it quiet much longer and I haven't even told my parents yet. It's all going to kick off and I don't want you getting, well, you know ... hurt."

"Do you like her...?"

Ryan shakes his head, "I ... I ... It's you Jess. I wanted you and me to go to Africa, or anyway, just be together, but now...." His head drops.

I look straight ahead and say nothing. What can I say? His secret is just as bad as mine. He's telling me it's over then. Once we get home, I'll never see him again, will I?

Now I have no one.

The rest of the journey is total misery. Ryan turns his phone back on and keeps texting, and he moves to the other side of the car. I don't want him next to me, but I do. I'm so confused. In the end I doze off. We arrive back on the

Island after eight and Max drops me at home. Sarah calls out about speaking later but I just mumble back at her. I don't want to talk to anyone.

The house is very quiet when I let myself in. Just the hall light on. Mum has left me a note on the kitchen table.

`Lasagne in the freezer. I've gone to`
`the clubhouse. veeve is out with friends.`
`we'll talk tomorrow. Mum`

What will Angela and the girls say when they find out that Mum's not minted anymore? They'll dump her so fast. And very soon Nana Hat is going to find out the truth, isn't she? I mean, who's going to pay the bills in her nursing home? Where will she go then?

But actually, I'm so relieved no one's home, and that there's no sign of Dad either, that the tears I've been holding in for hours start pouring down my face. I don't really care about Mum or Dad, or even Veeve. And there's nothing I can do for Nana. What I'm really crying about is Ryan and his terrible secret. I fell in love with him, didn't I?

I really, really needed him; needed to be loved and taken away. I can't get my head round it. I would never have thought in a million years that Ryan would do something like that. As I stumble upstairs all I can think is, Ryan's got another girl pregnant and he's dumped me.

I am so stuffed!

160

In my room I stand in front of the mirror. I have built-in wardrobes that go the full width of my room and the doors are all mirrors. I look such a mess. What happened to gorgeous, sexy Jess Jayne, chased by all the boys, envied by all the girls?

My hair's tangled like a bird's nest and I'm wearing Sarah's clothes, which don't go together. Everything's covered in mud. My face is streaked with tears and I'm wearing odd socks. I can't stand it. I pull everything off and go and stand in the shower for ages.

At least Mum left the central heating on and the house is warm. Gradually I stop crying and shaking and turn off the water. I wrap myself in my dressing gown, a towel over my dripping hair, go downstairs and make hot chocolate and toast.

I'm going to chill out in my bedroom for the rest of the evening, watch my TV and write my diary. At least I still have my diary.

sun nov 23

I thought it was me and Scott last summer and look what happened. Then I fell for Ryan and he's got a girl pregnant. Does he love me? My head's all over the place. Dad's not who he pretended to be all my life. Mum just cares about the girls. I thought I was going to die three months ago. I thought my life was really stuffed. But since then things have gotten SO BAD BAD BAD!!!!!!!!!!

Me and Ryan were going to run away together. What am I going to do now? Whatever, I'm going to need some money!!!!!!!!!!

Money. I hadn't really thought about that before but now I switch on my laptop to check my internet bank account. I flip through my diary for my password. It's on the fifteenth page in the middle of the first sentence – xheffalump618.

Veeve's password is so pathetic – hairband1. Dad says she'll get hacked if she doesn't look out.

But now I'm searching and searching through my account for my money and all I can see is a row of big fat zeros. This is insane! I know I had about £1700.00. All my birthday and Christmas money and the bonuses Dad would put in the account from time to time. "For when you start your own business, Jessie," he would say with a big grin.

Where's my money gone? Has my account been hacked? I must tell Dad. But where is he? I'm wondering what he'll say ... but then I stop. Dad's money's already gone. He said he'd lost everything. So where is my money?

I'm lying on my bed, staring at the laptop and I see the entry for two days ago, Friday 21 November....

| **Withdrawal** | £1785.48 |
| **Balance** | £0.00 |

Friday night. I came into the kitchen and Dad was counting out ten pound notes into Veeve's hand.

Oh My God! He stole it. My Dad stole my money to save his skin in front of Mum and Veeve.

I break down into uncontrollable, heaving sobs.

Chapter 24

"Wakey wakey, rise and shine!"

I come to and open one eye. There's a loud banging on the front door and the sound of a man's voice yelling. It's not a friendly voice. Through the gap in the curtains I can see the beginnings of a grey dawn.

The time on my clock is six fifty-six. I cried myself to sleep last night. I don't even remember hearing Mum and Veeve come in.

"Come on missus, open up!" The voice is really aggressive and there's more banging. It sounds like a huge fist pounding on the wood. Did Mum do the double lock last night?

"Mum!" Veeve is calling out in a frightened voice.

I push off the covers and pull on a hoody over my PJs.

Then I hear Mum saying, "All right, what on earth is all that noise for? Wait a minute, I'm coming."

I go to my bedroom door and look out into the corridor. Veeve is standing at the top of the stairs, peering down, her hair all mussed up. She's only got shorts and a vest on.

"What's going on?" I say. "Where's Dad?"

"Don't you know? Dad hasn't been home all weekend. He went off Friday night after you had that tantrum."

"You're the one who doesn't know anything," I say, rubbing my eyes. I still feel half asleep.

"Well Mum said it's all your fault he's gone."

"No, it's not, Veeve," I say, but my voice is drowned out by more banging.

"Coming?" I ask, but she doesn't move so I go downstairs.

Mum is fiddling about with keys and the door is shaking from the banging. She looks all confused and suddenly very small, as though she's swallowed something and shrunk to half her size.

I get an awful feeling inside me. Something's not right here, I think. Where's Dad? What's he done now? And then I think it's the police and I feel this huge mixture of fear and relief. It's over and *I* won't have to do all the explaining. At least I won't have to be the one to break Nana Hat's heart. Ryan pops into my mind for a moment, but I push the thought away. I can't think about being dumped right now.

I reach out and take the keys from Mum's hands, which are shaking. She doesn't stop me. "It's OK," I say quietly. "I'll speak to them."

I feel strangely calm as I unlock the door and open it. There's a huge bloke on the doorstep with two others behind him. Their heads are shaved and they've got ties and white shirts on under black bomber jackets. I was right, I think, it's the police.

"Bailiffs," says the man on the doorstep and suddenly his foot is in the door as if he thinks I'm going to slam it in his face. Then he's in the porch. Beyond him I see the other two men lift a metal sheet and go to the front window. A drilling starts up, as if they're boring into the brickwork.

"Hey," I say, but my voice is shaking. "Where's your warrant card?"

"We're not police, sweet'eart. Is Mr Fitzgerald home?"

Mum steps forward and says, "He's not here. Who are you and what do you want?"

"I see," he says, and there is something in his face that fills me with dread. He knew Dad wouldn't be here, I'm sure.

"We were here two weeks ago but no one answered," the man says. "That was the final warning, last chance. Mr Fitzgerald's had all the letters." He waves a piece of paper about in his hand.

I can see now that this man isn't a policeman. What is he then? What's a bailiff?

He hands Mum the paper and she stares at it.

Veeve comes downstairs, she's thrown on jeans and a jumper but her feet are bare. Her face is still a bit vague from sleep.

Mum and Veeve have no idea, do they? To be honest, I'm not too sure I do either. Why are these men here and what's Dad done now?

There's drilling and banging going on all round the house and the living room has gone very dark. "What are they doing?" I ask the man.

"Putting up the shutters so no one can get in," he says.

"Are you a security firm?" asks Veeve and I want to laugh out loud. This bloke doesn't care about our security. He wants Dad for something and it must be to do with money. But I still don't get it. Why put shutters around the house if Dad isn't here?

"No, sweet'eart, we've come for the house. Mr Fitzgerald had his chance to sort his debts but he didn't take it, did he? He's had all his warnings. We've been told to shut the house up today and you have to leave. It's being repossessed by the bank."

Mum's face has drained white. I feel sick and Veeve looks as if she's going to faint.

"Leave?" says Mum and her voice isn't much more than a whisper. "What do you mean, leave? This is my home."

"Mum! Get Dad, this is insane! Jess! Where's Dad? You know don't you, why don't you tell us!" Veeve is crying and shouting and she's collapsed onto the stairs. Mum is shaking and her arms are wrapped around her body and all I can think is that I've got to get them away from this man and tell them the truth about Dad.

I turn my back on the man and I say in this really urgent voice, "Mum, Veeve, you've got to listen, I've got something to tell you."

They both look up at me and there's such hope in their eyes I feel a stab in my tummy. They think I know how to sort this.

"Come into the kitchen, it's about Dad." I turn back to the man. "Give us a minute, all right?"

He looks at me and I think he realises I know something they don't.

He gives me a brief nod. "Fine," he says, and he goes off outside yelling to the other two men.

I walk towards the kitchen but Mum and Veeve don't follow me. So I turn back and snap, "Come on!"

Their eyes open wide but they follow me.

Once we get in the kitchen Mum starts on me, saying, "What's going on, Jess? What have you and your Dad been up to now, and why...."

"MUM!!" I yell in such a big voice that she stops midstream, her mouth open. I go over and put my arms on her shoulders, guide her to a chair and push her down onto it. "Just listen, OK, we haven't got much time. Veeve, please, for once, just listen."

Veeve is staring at me, her dark eyes rounded with fear. A tear trickles down her cheek but she nods.

I try to keep my voice calm as I tell them as quickly as possible how Dad has lost all his money, about the stealing from the wallets and the fraud with the credit card. They're staring and staring at me, but even they can see I'm not making all this up.

Then, just as I run out of breath, a wail escapes from Mum's mouth and then she's wailing and wailing and wailing and I'm so scared. I don't know what to do now.

I can hear the man coming back down the corridor. If we have to leave, surely we're allowed to get dressed and pack some stuff. We can come back for the rest later. But we're running out of time. Panic whips up through me.

So I do something I thought only happened on TV.

I slap Mum's face.

She stops mid-scream and there's a horrible silence in the room. Then the kitchen door opens and the man says, "Pack a bag, I can give you ten minutes, that's all, then the house will be shuttered and bolted. The gas and water's already cut off."

His face is like a plastic mask as he looks at us.

"Come on, Mum, Veeve," I'm pulling them up, pushing them towards the door. "Get upstairs." Then I say more quietly, "Pack some clothes, Mum, take your jewellery, and our passports. What else do we need?" I'm pushing them down the corridor and almost hauling them upstairs. I'm panting by the time we get to the top and still they are looking numb and frozen. "You've got to hurry up, you've got to do this."

"But what about Dad?" whispers Mum in a hoarse voice.

"He's gone, Mum. He's gone and he's left us with his mess. We've got to get out of here with as much as we can carry, and then we can look for him, can't we?"

That seems to get her going. She nods and says, "You're right, you're right, come on, Veeve, both of you, put on warm clothes, your boots, you'll need your boots, and we must take our winter coats, pack as much as you can in a suitcase."

Suddenly everyone springs into a sort of fevered action and we dash into our rooms. I look round for what I want, grab my diary, empty my drawers, sling clothes into my biggest sports bag, pull on jeans, three jumpers, thick socks and then we are all in the hallway, dragging our bags down the stairs.

The man is standing at the bottom, his arms folded, looking impatient. "Come on missus, look sharp, I ain't got all day, we got to get to Southsea in twenty minutes."

"When can we come back for the rest of our things?" says Mum. "And what about the furniture? I need to arrange a place in storage until we find somewhere to live."

The man shakes his head. "House clearance will sort it. Your husband had his warnings. He should have been to his bank months ago."

He turns and opens the front door and stands aside, waving his hand towards us. As I look out onto the drive I see a pickup truck has lifted up Mum's car and is driving away with it.

"My Toyota!" Mum screams, and pulling her case she rushes out of the door.

I look at the man.

He shrugs and says, "Owes money all round, don't he?"

"Come on, Veeve," I say, but she just stands there, tears pouring down her face. So I haul my bag onto my shoulder, grab the handle of her case in one hand and with the other hand I grab her arm and pull her out into the front garden.

We turn and look back at our house, our home. The windows are all covered with huge metal shutters and the place looks almost derelict now. How could this have happened in less than thirty minutes?

Chapter 25
Ryan

Monday morning. I'm at my work station trying to avoid Shelley, who's on scream mode, when Lee sends a text: **ive told dad. don't kum ovr or fone. dad mad** ☹

God!

My chest is pounding and I can hardly breathe. Is this a heart attack? Why didn't she wait for me? Don't I have a say in this? Not that I want to force her or anything. But God, psycho Wayne with an arsenal in his basement. He's going to kill me!

"You've only been in five minutes and you're already on the phone!" Shelley's spotted me and she's on me like a tornado. "I want to see your nose at that screen non-stop until lunchtime!"

I want to kill *her*.

I tap madly on the keyboard as Shelley goes past. When she's gone I look at what I've been typing. It's rubbish. I have to delete the whole lot and start again.

Lee's cousin, Denny, the one who brought her to the beach party, knows where I live. We hang out sometimes. He might tell Lee and she'll come over with her Dad. I tuck my phone under the keyboard shelf and type with one hand: **mate, heard from lee?**

I put my phone on silent and tuck it into my jeans, hoping I'll notice if it vibrates.

Lunchtime I go out to the High Street and check my phone. Denny's texted back: **yeah.**

What does that mean? But I don't want to ask him anything else. He'd give Lee my address if she asked, wouldn't he? I find myself walking automatically towards the camping shop to see Max. But then I stop. I don't want to see Max. He was stupid on the climbing trip, nearly killing James. How can I talk to him about the baby if I can't trust him with my own brother?

Mum and Dad got home just after Max dropped us off so there was no time to get cleaned up or anything. Mum went mad when she saw James's face. I was sure he was going to drop me in it as usual. But he didn't.

"I fell off my bike, Mum, don't make such a fuss. I'm fourteen not five."

"You could have concussion. Couldn't he?" she'd said to Dad.

Dad had just shrugged and taken the cases upstairs, calling over his shoulder, "I'm sure he's OK."

"Yeah, Ryan looked after me," James said and smiled at me. Amazing.

Mum had looked from me to James and back again but then she'd said, "Well, I'm so glad you boys got on over the weekend, let's hope it continues. I don't like it when you fight, you know."

"Yes Mum," we both said at the same time.

I finish work by four-thirty because I started early, but I could hardly concentrate all day. I don't know what to do for the best. Drive to Portsmouth and see Lee and her Dad? Tell my Mum and Dad?

Part of me is still desperate to ask Max, but all that's changed since the weekend. Trust's gone, hasn't it? I don't know who to turn to, and I'm missing Jess so much. Did I really need to tell her? Her face in the car all the way home was so numb and hurt. I moved away so that she didn't have to sit close to me and then I felt all cold and empty. Max didn't say anything when he dropped me off either. At least me and James are getting on. But when he finds out about the baby he'll know what a jerk I am.

When I get home there's a note on the kitchen table from Mum. She's gone to the supermarket and Dad's working late. The house is very quiet. It's gone five. James must be home. I go up to his bedroom and tap on the door.

"What?" he says.

"You OK?"

He doesn't answer and I turn away. Didn't last long, all that brotherly love, did it?

I go downstairs and make myself a cheese sandwich. I'm just about to go out to the garage when I hear the engine of a motorbike in the road, quite a powerful bike. I go into the front room and tweak the net curtains; I'm just in time to see a Kawasaki roadster pull up outside the front gate. The rider switches off the engine. He's wearing one of those helmets with a blacked-out visor and I can't see his face. He's a really big bloke and I can just see there's someone much smaller on the back of the bike.

Then he takes the helmet off. It's Wayne, and Lee is dismounting onto the pavement.

I drop the curtain in shock and throw myself on the floor. Has he seen me? Has he got a gun with him? I'm shaking and my armpits are prickling with sweat, just like when we were climbing. I creep up as far as the window sill and try to look under the net.

"You idiot, what you done now?" It's James.

"Shhh!" I hiss. My heart is pounding. "Get down."

James just stands there grinning. So I roll across the floor and pull him down. He nearly bangs his head again.

"Oi!" he yells out before I can get my arm round his neck.

"Shut up," I whisper.

He gets the message and stops struggling. I release my grip.

"What's up?" he whispers back.

"There's a bloke outside with a gun and I think he wants to kill me."

James laughs out loud and I clamp my hand over his mouth.

Then the doorbell goes. It's got this stupid ring that goes on forever and then repeats. Mum loves it. Drives the rest of us crazy.

James goes rigid under my hand and I let go. The bell rings again and then there's a single loud thump on the reinforced glass. James looks how I feel. Terrified.

"Bruv, you serious?" he says. I can't help noticing he's never called me bruv before.

174

I nod and we stay there on the floor. Wayne rings the doorbell again and we hear him yell, "I'm not going anywhere, open up," and he bangs on the glass again.

Then James whispers, "I'll go."

"Are you insane?"

"He won't know me; I'll pretend I've never heard of you."

Before I can stop him, he's on his feet, tucking his T-shirt into his jeans as he goes off down the hallway and opens the front door.

I want to push myself into the tiny cupboard under the stairs and lock myself in. I used to like hiding there when I was little; it was a nice, warm, safe place to be. I loved it when Mum came looking for me and stood outside the door calling, "Ryan, where are you?" Of course she knew I was there, but she joined in the game until I came out laughing.

"What?" I hear James say in a bored voice.

He's got a nerve, but perhaps he'll get rid of them, I think, with a little buzz of hope. I search my memory frantically. Did I tell Lee I have a little brother? I don't remember.

"We're looking for Ryan, your brother is it?" I hear Wayne say. His voice is so rough.

"Who?" says James.

"You know who, you little squirt. Your brother, Ryan. I want to see him, go get him."

James doesn't answer and Wayne yells, "Now!!"

I hear Lee give a little giggle and that does it. I'm not having Lee laugh at my brother.

I march down the hall but my knees almost give way

when I see Wayne. He's got something tucked under his arm, something long and thin in a sort of canvas cover. It looks like a gun. I knew it!

"Run, James!" I yell. "He's got a gun. Go on, run!"

James looks at me, his face twisted in fear, and then Wayne lets out this enormous hoot of laughter. "You stupid boys, what do you think I am? A hit man?" He pulls open the canvas and inside is a fishing rod.

I feel myself go deep red.

"Ryan?" says James, looking confused.

"I just want a word with you, son, I don't shoot *people*." Wayne is smiling at us and he doesn't look half as frightening as I thought.

"Are your Mum and Dad home?"

I lick my lips; my mouth has gone dry with fear. Then I say, "No."

"Well, tell them we came over to see them ... We've got to sort this out." He nods towards James, "I take it you haven't said anything yet?"

"About what?" says James.

I give him a push and say, "Go up to your room, I'll explain later."

Surprisingly he goes, throwing over his shoulder, "You better."

Once he's gone I say to Wayne, "I'll tell them, please, just give me a couple of days. My parents, you know, they'll take it quite hard."

"Tell me about it, lad, she's only sixteen, just a kid," says Wayne with a frown. "What were you thinking?"

Lee just stands there. She looks younger than James.

"To be honest," I say, "I haven't a clue."

Wayne gives me a long stare and then he says, "Takes two to tango, I suppose." He looks at Lee and then back at me. He raises his eyebrows and in that second I think he understands it's not all my fault.

"I haven't told her mother yet but Lee definitely doesn't want an abortion, do you love?"

Lee shakes her head.

Oh God! I feel my heart sink. She's decided to have it and I realise that I was clinging on to the hope that she would want to get rid of it. But then I think, What kind of a monster wishes his own baby dead? I feel so guilty I can't even bear to look at Lee.

"Whatever," I mutter, my eyes fixed on the ground. "I'll go along with whatever and I'll support her. But...."

I stop and Wayne says quietly, "I don't believe in shotgun weddings." Well, that's a relief. "You tell your parents today, right? Then we can take it from there, but get on with it, lad. We need to get this sorted. OK?"

"I will, I promise," I say.

Wayne gives me a nod and Lee smiles and waves. Then they turn and take off down the path, Lee skipping behind him like she did when we went to the park.

This is going to make her grow up quick. The thought makes me feel a bit sad. She seems so young.

I watch them drive away and then I close the front door and go up to James's room.

"When's she due?" he says. He's sprawled out on his bed surrounded by his schoolbooks.

He must have been listening at the top of the stairs, so there's no point in pretending. "I dunno, months. You going to tell Mum?"

He's silent, fiddling with one of his folders. It's really thick, stuffed with notes. He's always studying, except when he's having a go at me or he's out with his girlfriend. He could do anything he wants; he won't screw up his life like me, I think. Lucky little jerk.

"Bruv," he says in a quiet voice, "you didn't tell Mum about the accident and how stupid and big-headed I was on the rocks. You saved my life."

I lean against the doorpost and we're silent for a minute.

"Why didn't you tell me about the baby?" he says.

"Thought you'd just laugh at me and tell Mum."

He doesn't say anything and I turn to go.

Then he says, "Wait up." I stop. "You can trust me," he says. "I thought I was gonna die up there in the snow. Then you came for me. I thought you'd just leave me...."

"Never! You're my little brother."

He nods at me and we're quiet for a minute and then he says, "What're you going to do?"

"Dunno. I'm scared," I say honestly.

He nods sympathetically and I feel so guilty. I blamed James, didn't I? For teasing me about being gay and making me go and sleep with Lee. How stupid is that? It wasn't James's fault Lee got pregnant. It was mine.

Chapter 26
Jess

I wake up with a start, and I don't know where I am for a few moments. But then it all comes back to me and I get this horrible sinking feeling. I'm lying on a put-up bed in a tiny room, which Social Services have moved us into. It was only a few days ago that we left our lovely big house, but it feels like a lifetime. I thought my life couldn't get any worse when I was in hospital; I thought it couldn't get any worse when I saw Dad stealing from those wallets. Well, this time I really don't think it could.

Last Monday, me, Mum and Veeve had stood at the bus stop near our home, all of us crying. Veeve just sat down on the pavement. She looked like a puppet that had had its strings cut. I was so scared; I didn't know what to do. Mum didn't say anything, she just stood there, clutching the handle of her suitcase.

A bus appeared and I tugged at Veeve's arm, coaxing her, "Get up, come on, Veeve, get up." But she wouldn't move and the bus didn't stop. "Why didn't you put out your arm?" I yelled at Mum.

"I didn't think," she said. It was probably about a million years ago that Mum had last taken a bus.

We had to wait half an hour for the next one.

"What if someone sees the house?" Mum said. "What

will people think? Everyone's going to know that we've been evicted." She started to cry again.

"No one will see, Mum," I tried to soothe her. "No one ever comes along our road. And none of the neighbours know any of our friends." But I was annoyed that that was all she was worried about.

Finally, we all got on a bus and into town, but then we had no idea what to do. We stood on the High Street with all the shoppers going round us, avoiding our heap of bags. I didn't see anyone from school, which was a relief.

Mum kept saying, "What's he done to us? How could he do this?"

What I really wanted was to go to Ryan in the hospital, but I was scared he wouldn't speak to me. Imagine if he knew what had happened. And me and Ryan have no future anyway; he's having a baby with another girl.

In the end we went to Social Services.

Mum and Veeve cried the whole time we were in the offices. I had to fill in all the forms and tell them everything.

They sent us to this horrible little room in a flat above a bookies. They call it bed and breakfast. There was only one proper bed. They brought a put-up bed round later that day. The bathroom's down the corridor and we have to share it with other people. So gross.

Veeve cried all night.

We hardly went out the next day; we didn't want anyone to see us, and anyway we had almost no money. Mum went and tried to get some out with her card, but everything's been stopped. She just had a few quid in her purse.

Veeve wouldn't get out of bed at all – she lay under the covers all day. She wouldn't eat or drink anything and she wouldn't speak to me. I didn't know what to do and Mum was so distracted, worrying about money and how to get out of this horrible room.

The second night, Veeve took the pills. We only just got to her in time.

She must have grabbed the packets of paracetamol when she packed her bag before we left. Mum found her in that horrible bathroom, lying on the floor, surrounded by empty blister packs. Mum went crazy, like when the bailiffs came. I had to dial 999 on the old Nokia I'd borrowed from Nana Hat. Mum and Veeve's phones have stopped working now too. Their contracts must have finally been cancelled.

The doctors in Accident and Emergency told us if we had left Veeve a few more hours she could have done some serious damage. They pumped her stomach, but they wouldn't let her come home with us. Well, I think that's a good thing. To be honest she's better off in hospital, isn't she?

They moved her to a psychiatric ward on Wednesday. She won't talk to anyone; she hasn't spoken since we left the house and went to the bus stop. The doctor says she's traumatised.

I blame myself. I should have seen it coming. Veeve isn't really a strong person, not like Nana Hat and Nana Hat's mother. And, well, me, I suppose. I've realised that. I have to be strong; someone has to sort things out.

I should have realised how bad Veeve was, should have kept an eye on her. What if my sister had died?

We go and see her every day and the ward is very bright and cheerful. She has her own room and there are other young people there. But none of them speak or even meet your eyes. Veeve just lies in bed, she won't get dressed and the nurses say they can't get her to eat much. They look in on her all the time.

Veeve tried to commit suicide, didn't she? I just can't get my head round it.

"What if she never eats again?" I said to Mum yesterday as we were leaving.

"They'll put her on a drip this weekend if she doesn't start eating," said Mum.

I know what that feels like.

I managed to get a job yesterday and I've already done one shift. Washing up in a restaurant on the edge of town, cash-in-hand and no questions asked. I did six hours and got paid £20.00, not even the minimum wage. But we're desperate, aren't we?

"We've got to look after ourselves," I told Mum after we left Veeve in the hospital that first day.

"I hate leaving her there," was all Mum said.

I did too. Veeve looked so small and pathetic lying in bed in a hospital gown. Mum and I sat up with her all night and we were both exhausted. We hadn't had anything to eat all day. But when Mum looked in her purse it was empty – we didn't even have the bus fare to get back to our horrible room. We had to walk all the way in the rain.

That was when I knew I had to get a job or we'd just starve to death.

When I arrive at work there's a sink full of pans to wash up. I think the other kitchen hands leave me the worst ones.

I start on the pans and bang the pots around in the sink. The head chef yells at me for making too much noise and I glare back, thinking what a blockhead he is.

Only that makes me think of Ryan and I get such an aching inside me. I haven't spoken to him since the climbing weekend. I would have called if we hadn't lost the house. Too much has happened since Sunday, even though he's called me loads.

I love him, I really do, but he's going to be a Dad and he's got enough on his plate without me, the world's biggest loser, with a depressed sister, pathetic Mum and worst of all, a criminal Dad.

Dad has no idea what has happened to Veeve. Doesn't he care about us? He must know by now that we've had to leave the house. We could be living out of a cardboard box for all he knows.

If only he would get in touch. We don't know where he is, and have no way of finding him. But then, maybe we're better off without him.

I've heard Mum calling Dad from Nana Hat's phone – leaving voicemail after voicemail for him – when she thinks I'm asleep. "Please Ronny, please ring me, I'll understand, just get in touch."

It's awful, it makes me feel so sad and really lonely. At

least if Veeve was around we could have a good shouting match about sharing the bathroom, or who grabbed the last bit of toast. I wish I'd packed a little radio when we left so I could turn up the music and drown out Mum's weepy voice. But there was no time to think, no time for anything with those bailiffs banging the shutters over the windows and telling us to get out.

Dad never answers his phone, never rings her back. We haven't heard a peep from him since before the climbing weekend.

I hate him! I think. I bang the pots loudly in the sink, ignoring the head chef yelling at me to shut up.

Chapter 27

Ryan

I'm under the van when I hear the motorbike pull up. My stomach does a double flip. It's Wayne with Lee. Mum's invited them to Sunday tea to discuss the baby.

It's been a whole week since I last saw Jess. I miss her so much. I really did love her. Now I've got to get through this stupid afternoon.

"Ryan," Dad calls, and I pull myself out slowly and get up.

"Yeah," I say, smearing my hands down my jeans. I've got grease on my hands and I'm wearing old jeans with holes in the knees. But I'm not trying to impress anyone; they already think I'm the scum of the earth.

"Go and get cleaned up, we'll hold the fort."

"What for?" I mutter, but he gives me such a look I don't argue.

I slip into the house and up the stairs before anyone sees me. I go into the bathroom and lock the door.

It was so awful telling Mum and Dad last week. Especially Mum. She had her *Can't cook, Won't cook* apron on and she lifted it up to her face and cried into it. She didn't make any noise but when she took the apron down her eyes were all wet. Dad put his arm round her and said, "Oh Ryan." It cut me to the bone.

I looked across at James as we all sat round in the kitchen and he smiled supportively.

"Whatever were you thinking?" Mum had said.

"What about protection?" said Dad. "I thought they did all that in school these days."

"They do," I said. "I just didn't think."

"No, well, that's the trouble," said Dad. He looked more sad than angry but his voice rose a bit and I felt tears well up. James raised his eyebrows to the ceiling and that helped.

"What about you?" said Mum, turning on James, "Did you know about this, this ... Lee and a baby? Why didn't you say something? Do you think it's funny?"

James couldn't help smiling but I knew it was nerves. "No," he said and pulled his face into a frown. "Anyway, it's not my fault, why're you getting at me?"

"We're not son, we're just upset. Not sure what to do, really," said Dad and I couldn't bear the lost look on his face.

I stare at my face in the bathroom mirror and try to rub a grease spot off my cheek. I so wish I could turn back the clock.

If only I hadn't gone to that stupid party. There was another girl I'd quite fancied. If I'd gone with her instead of Lee then I wouldn't have been part of Lee's stupid game to keep up with her friends and sleep with the first loser she got her hooks into. That's me, Ryan O'Neill, the world's biggest loser. Mum's words keep ringing in my ear: "You can forget all about that trip to Africa, Ryan. You've got responsibilities, now."

Mum had banged the flat of her hand down hard on the table and we'd all jumped. "Sell that van and start saving.

186

Children cost a lot of money!"

I felt like my life was seeping out of my trainers onto the lino. Sell the van? No way! It was then I realised what this has all been about. Going to Africa was some sort of crazy dream, a way to escape because I hadn't passed my exams, gone to college. Going on a road trip sounded exciting, and anyway Jess had wanted to come too, hadn't she? Only now I could see that she was trying to escape too. None of it was real.

But what I really loved was getting under the van, learning how to fix it, getting my hands dirty. I like problem solving, but not climbing up a rock face. I want to fix engines and cars. If I sell the van I'll have nothing left. All my dreams smashed up. I felt tears in my eyes again.

Then Dad had said in a quiet but firm voice, "Hold on, love. Ryan knows what he's done and all credit to him. He's said he's going to stick by the girl and make sure the baby gets everything it needs." He turned to me and put his hand on my shoulder, "I'm proud of you saying that. I wouldn't have been happy if you'd just ignored it and not told us."

There was a bit of a silence and then Mum said, "Well, only what I would have expected from our Ryan. He's always been a good boy."

She was wiping the last of the tears away from her eyes, but I could see that she didn't hate me.

I scrub away at my greasy hands and sprinkle some water on my hair to smooth it down. I suppose I should make a bit of an effort with Lee's family, if only for Mum's sake. Maybe that way she won't see me as a complete loser. Not like Max.

I finally decided to go and see him in the camping shop in the week. James said I should and he was right, the climbing accident wasn't *all* Max's fault. So I said we were all responsible and Max had shrugged and said OK. Then I told him about Lee and the baby.

"You are joking!" he'd blasted out. "Denny's cousin?"

"Keep your voice down," I'd said, ducking my head with embarrassment. There were a couple of blokes from the Post Office having coffee in the tent and I could see they were listening in.

"Mate," said Max, "hope she was worth it." He was shaking his head and clipping quick-draws to a climbing harness which was laid out on the counter, preparing for another carefree climbing weekend.

"Didn't you tell her to get rid of it?"

I stared at him and I wanted to say, "You think it's so easy, like climbing a Severe, just a problem to solve. Watch your feet, push up, do a bit of jamming and you're there. On top of the world and no one can touch you." But I didn't say anything.

This – Lee and the baby – is real life. Max might be older than me but right at that moment, *he* sounded like a little kid. Like James before he grew up a bit this week.

"It's not my business to tell Lee anything," I said, and my voice was really cold. Max gave me a sideways look. "I told her it was her decision and I would support her, whatever."

That hit home. Max dropped his head and started to fiddle about with his harness again.

Stuffed

"See you around," I said and left the shop. He didn't call after me.

I made a mistake thinking Max knew all the answers. I'm the one who has to sort this out.

There's a bang on the bathroom door and I hear James yell, "They're waiting."

I take one last look in the mirror and unlock the door. James is standing there in a white T-shirt and black jeans.

"You're not wearing that?" he asks, looking at my dirty old jeans. He shoves me into my room and starts raking through my wardrobe.

"This and this," he says and throws a blue shirt and cream trousers over to me.

"Too posh," I say.

"Mum says you need to make a good impression."

He's right, I think, I don't want to upset her even more. I change my clothes.

When we get downstairs there's an embarrassing silence in the living room. Mum has the best teapot out and she's pouring tea, and Dad's following her around with the sugar bowl. Everyone's spending ages stirring their tea and taking sips, and arranging napkins awkwardly on their laps. All the armchairs are taken and there's only a tiny space on the sofa. But then I'd be jammed up close to Lee. So I sit on the edge of the TV cabinet.

"Go and get a couple of chairs from the kitchen," Mum snaps and James ducks back out the door.

189

"You must be Ryan," says a youngish-looking woman sitting next to Lee on the sofa. She looks like she could be Lee's big sister. She has long, straggly hair, the same colour as Lee's, and she's just as small and thin. They're both wearing yellow T-shirts and skinny jeans. "I'm Terri, Lee's mum," says the woman. "You look younger than I thought, doesn't he Wayne?"

Wayne is silent, stirring his tea.

Terri seems nervous and says, "Oh look, you've got a lava lamp, Jen, is it?"

Mum nods and says, "James and Ryan bought it for us last Christmas."

We got it in a charity shop. It was kind of a joke, but Mum actually quite likes it. We think it's a bit naff.

"That's a nice present," says Terri. "Me and Nick, that's my partner," she gives Lee a little pat and Lee goes red, "we've got a lava lamp."

"All right, that's enough," says Wayne in a gruff voice. "We're not here to discuss him."

Even I go red, but Terri doesn't look bothered. She dips a chocolate biscuit in her tea and offers it to Lee, "Come on, *baby*, you're eating for two now."

Lee frowns and shakes her head.

"Morning sickness," says Terri, looking round the room. No one meets her eye. She seems pretty dumb, like Lee. Oh God, does that mean the baby will be dumb too? I'm trying to avoid Lee's eyes but it's really hard, she's right opposite me.

Wayne and my Dad are eyeing each other up and down.

James is swinging on his chair. He's got three pieces of cake on his plate and he's dropping crumbs on the carpet.

"Sit still, James," snaps Mum, fussing round, tidying the coffee table. I can see she's nervous too but I don't know what to do.

Then Dad folds his arms and says to Wayne, "Ryan tells me you shoot."

Wayne nods, "Done a bit, amateur competitions, you know."

Dad looks impressed.

"He won the club bronze," says Lee and everyone looks at her. I'd forgotten how tinny her voice is.

I think of Jess, her cool voice, her lips kissing me when she lay down full length on me after the accident and then I remember how I pushed her off, terrified. I never got a chance to properly explain, did I?

"Boys and their toys," Terri's saying, rolling her eyes, and she winks at Mum. "Me and my mates go bingo, how about you Jen?"

"We don't hold with gambling," says Mum, and that feels good.

At least my parents are proper grown-ups, not like Terri and Wayne with their guns and their bingo. No wonder Lee's so immature.

Then Wayne gives a cough and says, "The way I see it is this." I wonder if he's going to tell us to get the baby adopted so he and Terri can get on with their stupid lives. "Ryan and Lee got their whole lives ahead of them," he goes on. "Lee's got to do her exams and Ryan, I don't know what you do, mate, but you're only, what, seventeen?" I nod. "So between us we've got to sort out the baby and make sure these kids don't muck up their lives any further."

Mum and Dad exchange glances. Terri helps herself to another slice of cake. Is she even listening?

"So what are you thinking, Wayne?" says Dad.

"Lee stays with me, we bring up the baby, Ryan's the Dad, gets his name on the birth certificate, proper like, and he shares in the responsibility. Come over whenever you want, mate, kids need their Dads, right?" My Dad gives a firm nod.

"We will help with childcare," says Mum.

"Yeah," Terri chips in, "and me and Jen can babysit anytime, have a girls' night in with a few cans?" says Terri with a loud laugh.

"Mum!" says Lee, and suddenly she sits up and says, "Me and Ryan are the parents, it's up to us to decide who babysits."

I'm quite surprised, I didn't think she had a thought in her head about all this, but as I stare at her I can see she's got quite a determined line to her chin as she sticks it up in the air.

"What do you have to say for yourself, lad," says Wayne.

Loads, actually, I think. I want to fix my van and drive it to Africa, be able to say I've done something with my life and now, well now it's all about the baby.

And suddenly I realise what I really want to do. I think I saw it that day on the rocks when James fell and I started to patch him up. I'm like Dad, good with my hands, I don't need to go to uni and I'm really good at problem solving.

"I want to be a mechanic," I blurt out and everyone stares

at me. I wait for James to give a hoot of laughter.

But actually what he says is, "Yeah, good for you." Mum and Dad are beaming at me and Wayne rubs his hand across his forehead and says, "Well, that's a surprise, mate. I thought you was one of them dropout types. Lee says you left school without no exams."

"I got five GCSEs," I protest.

Wayne gives me a hard look and then he says, "Lee is going to do A-Levels, she's very clever."

I'm really surprised. But now I look at her and there's something in her expression, a sort of serious look in her eyes I haven't noticed before. Basically, I've never really looked at her properly. Not like I did with Jess, drinking her in, never getting enough of her, even when I had to push her away. Will Jess ever forgive me?

"Lee's predicted all stars in her exams...." says Terri.

"*A* stars, Mum," says Lee.

"She'll be going to uni in a couple of years, wants to be a teacher, don't you, baby?" Terri goes on and Lee goes very red.

Then Lee says, "I'm sorry, Ryan, sorry I got you into all this trouble. But I couldn't get rid of it, it's not right. My Mum and Dad will help us and...."

"... so will mine," I say fiercely, "and you don't have to say sorry, it was both our faults. Now we've just got to get on with it."

There's a silence in the room and Mum and Dad are exchanging looks again. Terri picks at the crumbs on her plate and Lee seems to slip back into little girl lost, playing with her hair.

Then James gives a loud burp and Mum shrieks, "James!"
That's done it, I think, Mum's going to go mad.

But then Wayne laughs and Dad laughs a bit too, and Terri starts to giggle. Even Mum's face breaks into a smile.

James says to me, "Kitchen?"

I look at Lee and she looks a bit surprised and then her face splits into a really nice, big smile. Maybe the baby will have a smile like that.

Chapter 28
Jess

The Pit Bull downstairs is barking and growling again. Thank goodness Veeve is still in hospital. She's terrified of dogs and I don't know how she'll cope when they send her home to this place. Social Services moved us out of the bed and breakfast after a week so at least we've got a proper flat now. The Social said we're lucky: because of Veeve, and because we only need one bedroom, they managed to bump us up the list. I never knew that's what Social Services do.

Suddenly there's a high-pitched squeal and then a whimpering. They must have kicked it again. I check my eye-liner in the bathroom mirror. It's gone a bit wonky – even I'm scared of the dog.

The flat goes quiet now the dog's been silenced. All I can hear is the steady drip from last night's rain still landing in the bucket in the hallway. Mum stayed in all day yesterday, again, waiting for someone to come and fix the leak, but she has an interview this morning ... Another night with a leaky roof.

The people downstairs with the Pit Bull are a bit weird, but at least we've all got a proper bed now.

I want to snuggle back under my blanket, it's so cold, but I can't. I've got a shift at the restaurant today and I want to get to the library first and go on Facebook. I drag myself out of bed and throw on my clothes. The bath is cracked so we wash in the sink, but I can't be bothered this morning.

As I go into the hallway I glance at the mat. Maybe there'll be a card from someone but there's nothing. No one knows we're here. They don't even bother to deliver free newspapers to these flats. I wonder if anyone will remember it's my birthday today.

Nana Hat will, but I haven't seen Nana since the eviction. Mum's rung her a few times. She says Nana is all right. Mum had to call her to find out if she'd seen Dad. And then Mum had to tell her about Veeve, so I know she'll be worried sick. I want to go and see her but I can't face it. I don't know what to say about Dad and everything.

I guess she knows it all by now, and if she was going to have a heart attack over it, she would have, wouldn't she? I imagine her voice saying, "Mother always told us, what don't kill you makes you strong."

I don't know how much longer I can be strong. It's my sixteenth birthday today and Dad knows it. He *has* to get in touch today, or I will *never* speak to him again. Feeling pumped up, I go into the little kitchen to face Mum.

"I've made a pot of tea," she says. "But there's no milk." She said that yesterday morning too. We've been so busy, sitting with Veeve, or out looking for jobs, that we never seem to have milk, or bread, or much else for that matter.

She's scrabbling around in a drawer and then she pulls out a bag and hands it to me. "Happy birthday, Jess darling. It's not much but...."

Her voice trails off and we stand there staring at each other. I'm sure she's thinking the same as me. Of all the happy times we used to have on birthdays, the huge breakfasts, the presents, and sometimes outings to a show in London with dinner afterwards and a night in a hotel. Dad splashed the cash, and we all had such a good time.

All over now.

There are tears in Mum's eyes as she holds out the bag. Her skin is so pale and she looks like she's lost weight. I can't help thinking of my last birthday in school, with all my friends, surrounded by people. I got loads of cards. Only I haven't been back to school since the eviction. I can't face it. I thought the Social would snoop about but they don't seem to have done anything about it yet and term ends this week. I don't care. Mum and me just take one day at a time now.

I look at Mum's sad face. I have to try and cheer her up. "Thanks, Mum," I say with a cheerful smile.

That seems to help. She shakes herself a bit and says, "I'm going to see Veeve now, and I've got my interview at ten. I've got a good feeling about this salon." She pours the tea and dusts some crumbs off the shabby little table.

I open the bag. There's a homemade card, a chocolate bar, and some hair stuff, which I know is from the pound shop. Now *I* feel like crying.

"All right?" she says.

I nod, but there's such a lump in my throat I can't speak.

"Don't *you* go all quiet on me."

Like Veeve, I think. It's weird that she's the one in hospital

197

now, getting all the attention. She just couldn't cope with losing everything. Neither can Mum really, but once Veeve broke down, Mum made an effort to keep going. And I just get on with it; don't have a choice really, do I?

Mum's stopped cleaning the table and she's looking at me so I paste on another smile and say, "Chocolate! Thanks, Mum."

Then I give her a hug. "Good luck with the interview."

I glance at my watch. The library will be open in a few minutes, but it's a twenty-minute walk so I'd better get going. Have to be in the kitchen by eleven for the middle shift.

"I'm off now, Mum, give Veeve my love," I say, pulling on my coat.

As I go down the shaky wooden staircase to the ground floor I look round anxiously for the Pit Bull. No sign. That's a relief. I've been keeping a biscuit in my pocket, just in case. He hasn't tried to bite me yet but there's always a first time.

The wind is whipping in straight from the sea this morning and it cuts through my coat as I turn onto the road. It feels even colder today, maybe it's going to snow in time for Christmas – but that thought doesn't cheer me up. What's the point of Christmas this year? Dad's disappeared, Mum's a wreck and Veeve's in hospital. I don't ever remember not looking forward to Christmas.

The wind is blowing hard and it makes me think of that rock climbing weekend, when James fell and Ryan went up to get him and it started to snow. Wouldn't it be lovely if Ryan came past in his camper van right now and gave me a lift to the library?

It's still such a long way to walk; I never used to walk anywhere. I wish I hadn't left my bus pass in the house. At least my brand new National Insurance card was tucked into my passport. I remember being so excited when it came in the post. Like I was a proper grown-up, very nearly sixteen. I didn't know what was up ahead, did I?

Neither did Ryan. He doesn't even know it's my birthday today.

If only me and Ryan could drive off together in his camper van, right now. But instead, he's got a baby coming and I've got to be Supergirl for Mum and Veeve and Nana Hat. Otherwise we're all properly stuffed.

It's warm in the library and the assistant takes one look at me and gets me a hot chocolate from the machine. She gives me hot drinks for free when the head librarian isn't looking. I left my laptop at the house as well, and anyway we can't afford broadband. We can't afford anything anymore.

It's Jess Jayne's birthday today.
Hello Kitty Happy Birthday hunniiii love you ♥♥♥
Sarah Jayne Lewis ring me when you get back you're legal now babeeee ☺ !!!!
Karl Rees Have an amazing day. Lindy says Hi.
Alix Miller Happy Birthday from me and Samir
Emily Jayne Brown Haaaaaaaaaappy Birthday!!!!!!!!!!!!! ♥♥♥♥♥♥♥♥♥
Madonna Bling Hi! how r u guys btw Happy Birthday

Facebook is the only place where it's my birthday. I've said I've gone to Tunis with my family as a special treat, so they won't expect an answer. That's the thing about the Internet. You can say whatever you want. No one tells the truth on Facebook. I sip my hot chocolate and cruise around looking at everyone's photos. They're all having so much fun. I feel like an old woman, worrying about work and money.

I didn't have any breakfast so I rummage around at the bottom of my bag for my birthday chocolate bar. My fingers close round my diary. I carry it everywhere these days, like a talisman. But I haven't written in it since we left home. I pull it out and turn to a clean page. I've got a few minutes before I leave for work and I've got such an aching inside me I'll burst if I don't do something. I really thought Dad would get in touch on my birthday but I don't have any messages from him.

dec 17
Today I'm sixteen but I'm not sweet/happy/drunk. I looked on the mat for cards this morning, which was so stupid. Nothing from Dad. Nothing from Ryan; even more stupid.
They don't know where I am, and anyway they both dumped me.
I HATE MY DAD!!!!!!!!!!!!

But I loved Ryan. He was so sweet and gentle. Ryan will make a great Dad. Maybe I could go round and see the baby one day.

My phone rings. It's Mum.

"Hi," I say.

"Veeve's OK but she still won't speak," she sighs. "They won't let her home yet."

"OK."

"But I got the job – three mornings a week! It's a start I suppose, seven pounds twenty an hour. Still, there's one good thing, the girls will never come in. It's such a dump."

I don't say anything. Who cares about the girls? Who cares about anything? I'm sixteen today and look at us. Homeless, penniless, living on benefits, doing our washing in the sink because we can't afford the launderette.

"Jess, are you there?" She sounds frightened, like she does most of the time these days.

"Yes, don't worry, it's all going to be fine, Mum. I get paid today and once you start work we'll be OK again. We'll get some nice stuff for the flat and then it'll all be sorted for when Veeve comes home."

When I get to work no one speaks to me as usual, so I can't even tell them it's my birthday. There's a huge pile of dishes left over from breakfast and they're thick with grease. I hate this job so much. Will I ever get back to school and get my qualifications? I can't wash up for the rest of my life.

God! I didn't realise how *useless* Mum is. She didn't even know how to use the electric meter in the flat. Dad spoilt her so much that she's forgotten how to survive without him and his credit cards.

"Jessica Fitzgerald?"

I look around, wiping the sweat and soap suds off my forehead. It's the manager. I didn't think he even knew my name.

"Yes," I say.

He looks me up and down as if I'm something the dog dragged in and then he says, "Some bloke's asking for you in the restaurant."

"Who?" I say. But my heart gives a little leap. Maybe it's Ryan.

"He didn't say. Tidy yourself up before you go out front," he snaps, and then he turns on his heel and walks off.

My hair is all straggly and coming out of the hairnet they make me wear. My jeans and T-shirt are wet and have stains on them from washing the pans. I go into the little toilet, which stinks of the waiters' pee, and stare in the mirror. I pull my hairbrush out of my bag and brush down my hair. My face looks thin and pale and there are dark circles under my eyes. I pull on my jacket with the furry hood.

My heart's thumping as I walk the long corridors through the back end of the kitchens to the main restaurant. As I go through the side door and onto the carpeted floor I see a shape silhouetted against the huge windows.

But it's not Ryan.

It's Dad.

Chapter 29
Ryan

I check Facebook at the hospital when Shelley goes on her lunch break. It only takes me a minute. I've got five friends: Max, Sarah, James, Lee and Mum.

It's a good way to speak to Lee. We both hate speaking on the phone, so we just message each other. We're discussing names for the baby at the moment. She likes Memphis for a boy, after Elvis's birthplace. I've told her no way.

If I'm honest I think Facebook is stupid, but it's the only way I can think of to find Jess. I found out last night that it's her birthday today so I'm going to send her a Friend request at lunch time. I haven't before because I was hoping she'd see I'd joined, and contact me first.

Max showed me how to do it. He came into the hospital a couple of weeks ago.

"Mate," he said.

I looked up from my computer to see him leaning over reception, his black beanie pulled down low over his forehead. His eyes looked scared. I've never seen him scared before.

"Not *here*," I hissed, looking about for Shelley.

Max glanced over his shoulder and back again, gave me a quick nod and said, "Starbucks, I'll wait all day if I have to."

Then he was gone and I felt happy and worried all at the same time.

It took me almost an hour to get away but he was still there, flicking through a climbing magazine.

"He starts straight in, talking away in this rapid voice," Mate, I can't believe I was so stupid when you told me about Lee and the baby. I wouldn't blame you if you never spoke to me again."

He stared at me and I thought, that took some bottle. He's proud, Max, and he's older than me.

I stuck my hand out, "Put it there, mate."

He looked at my hand for a second and then he gave me a broad grin and grabbed it. We shook hard and I felt sort of manly and quite grown-up.

But that's me now. I *am* a grown-up, whether I'm ready or not. Lee's having the baby and I'm starting my mechanics course after Christmas. I have to set a good example to the baby.

Max was well impressed. "You going to college, man. I always said you had a brain. Not like me."

I went a bit red and said, "You're a climber."

"Yeah, well," he muttered. "Doesn't pay the bills, does it?"

We were quiet for a bit and then he said, "How's Jess?"

So I told him what we said in the car on the way back from the climbing trip, how she hadn't answered her phone to me since then and he phoned Sarah there and then. She told him Jess's family had gone on holiday to Tunis. She never mentioned it to me. Apparently Jess had put it up on Facebook just before they went.

204

"Don't know anything about Facebook," I said.
"I'll show you," Max said.

I've rung Jess loads, but she never answers. If she's in Tunis I suppose she wouldn't answer. But why didn't she tell me she was going? But then why would she? Last time I saw her, I told her I was having a baby with another girl.

Friend request sent on Facebook.
New message
To Jess Jayne
Happy Birthday, Jess! Please be my friend and let me know what you're up to.

I still haven't heard from Jess when I finish work so I go and get a birthday card and walk round to the camping shop.

"Can you text Sarah," I say to Max, "get Jess's address for me?" I hold up the card. It says, Sweet Sixteen Today.

The address is where all the posh houses are but I always knew she was minted.

After work I go home and get the van. I'm still doing it up at the weekends. It's the only thing that's kept me sane over the past few weeks.

Dad had to work hard on Mum, but in the end she agreed I could keep it. "You'll need it when the baby comes, I suppose," she said grudgingly, "and to practice on for your course."

Mum hasn't quite forgiven me yet. We sort of dodge round each other at home and sometimes I hear her crying in the bedroom. One night I heard Dad say, "Hush there, he's a good lad," but I couldn't hear what she said back. I feel bad most of the time anyway.

James's girlfriend, Pippa, saw me last weekend working on the van and hooted, "Still under that heap of rust?"

"Hey," said James as I stood there with a spanner in my hand. "Don't you disrespect my bruv."

We exchanged looks and Pippa tossed her head. At least I've got James on my side.

He can't wait to be an uncle.

"I'm sorting out all my old toys. Do you think she'll like Lego?" he said.

"How do you know it's a girl?" said Dad.

"Well, we don't need any more boys, do we?" said James and even Mum gave a bit of a smile.

Things will get better at home, I suppose, and Lee's Dad just wants me to do my bit. He's OK mostly, very fair.

But I miss Jess so much. Being without Jessica Fitzgerald feels like I have a great hungry space inside me.

When I get to the address the house is on this sort of private street, very quiet, no one else around, but I think Sarah must have made a mistake. It's a huge detached house with one of those drives that go in one side and out the other in a sort of curve, with a double garage I'd give my right arm for. But all the windows are covered with metal shutters.

I don't know what to do so I ring Max. "I think she must have moved," I say.

"Why?"

The place is all shut up, there are metal sheets bolted over the front door and all the windows. Where've they gone?"

"Weird," says Max. "Sheets of metal over the windows?" I hear his Dad call something out in the background and then he says, "My Dad says that means the bailiffs have been in."

"You what?"

"The bank has taken the house – they must be in debt and they've been chucked out."

God! So where is Jess? And where is her Dad? Maybe this is what she's been hiding from me.

Chapter 30
Jess

"Hi, Jess."

I don't know what to say. I've imagined this moment a million times since we got thrown out of the house, but now all I can do is stand here and stare at my Dad. He looks so weird. He's wearing dark suit trousers but a lighter jacket and the pockets are all baggy. His hair is so long it keeps falling in his eyes, and he looks like he hasn't shaved. Those aren't his clothes. Dad always wears designer suits and has his hair styled at Johns, the best place on the Island for men.

"How are you?" Even his voice sounds strange, all croaky. "And your Mum and Veeve?" There's a bit of a hopeful light in his eyes.

"Veeve's in hospital," I say.

The light flickers out.

Then I hear someone cough loudly behind me, and turning I see the manager glaring. He doesn't want two rejects like us cluttering up his restaurant.

"Come on," I mutter, and I push out of the glass double doors and walk off down the road.

Dad comes up alongside me and says in a strained voice, "What happened to Veeve?"

"She took an overdose after we got chucked out of the house."

He stops dead in the street and whips round to face me. "God, Jess! I can't believe it. She tried to...to...."

"... kill herself," I finish, and he flinches at the sarcasm in my voice. I feel a little pang but then I think he deserves it.

There's a few seconds while he pulls himself together and then he says, "Come on, I have to see her."

He wants to take off, dragging me with him and the look on his face is so stricken I almost weaken. But then I picture actually taking him to see Veeve. She's so fragile, I can't risk it.

"Not a good idea," I say.

"But how is she? Is she OK? I need to speak to the doctors. Are they taking proper care of her?"

"She's alive. They pumped her stomach. She's not talking though."

He groans. "My poor little girl. When did it happen? This week?" He grabs my arm, almost roughly, and says, "Let's go, and where's your Mum? Is she OK?"

I shake his arm off and almost spit in his face. "OK? How can she be OK? You disappear and leave her with nothing, we get kicked out of our home and then her eldest daughter tries to kill herself. Mum's in bits, that's how she is!"

Dad says in a hoarse whisper, "Is she in hospital too?"

I stand there for a moment, shoulders hunched, hands in my pockets, trying to will myself to walk away and leave him. Let him see how it feels.

But Dad starts up again, "Where are you living? You can at least tell me that, Jess? What happened after you left the house? Please, Jess, I need to know your Mum is OK."

I can't ignore him, so I say grudgingly, "She's OK. But she's hopeless, she couldn't even work the electric meter. You spoilt us Dad, you spoilt all of us."

His head drops and he says, "I'll make it up to you all. I promise, Jessie, you'll see."

I snort. I don't need any more promises or lies. Look where it got us last time, hiding everything from Mum and Veeve and then I had to sort the mess out.

"How did you find me?"

Dad shoves his hands in his pockets and says, "I drive a taxi now. I had a fare to the restaurant, saw you leaving."

"When?"

"Yesterday, I didn't know if you ... well, I slept on it and decided to come over today."

I don't say anything. Dad turns his head to stare down the street and when he looks back his face seems so tired, thinner than I remember, but there's a steely look in his eyes.

"I do understand, Jessie, really I do and I've come to find you to put things right, for you and your Mum and for Veeve."

He's speaking very quietly and his voice is so gentle and well, honest sounding. I feel a bit of my anger melting. Just one little corner.

We stand together for a few minutes and the traffic roars past us up to the lights. I see the manager come out of the restaurant and stare down the street at us. He taps the watch on his wrist. I'll lose my job if I stay out, but I can't walk away from Dad now.

Dad says, "I know I've let you down, Jessie, I've let you all down."

I look up into his eyes, the same colour as mine and Nana Hat's, and I can't help wondering who has let who down.

"Have you forgotten Nana Hat?" I say.

"No, never," he says. "I have a lot of making up to do. I've been looking all over for you. I've got a job now, my taxi's parked round the corner. I can look after you all again. I've gone over and over it in my head. I know what I've done, Jessie, and I've come to tell you that."

I've never heard him speak this way before, he was always joking, or handing out twenty pound notes from his wallet like they were sweets. Me and Veeve just took it all for granted. Why wouldn't we? We didn't know any better.

But then I think, wasn't that part of the problem? We all took Dad for granted. Mum, Veeve and me expected Dad to give us everything we wanted. I don't ever remember him saying no, and if he tried to say we had to wait for something, we'd go mad, or tease him or needle away at him until we got what we wanted.

None of us knew where to draw the line. I mean, me and Veeve, we're not babies, are we?

I remember one Friday we came home from school, I was fourteen and Veeve was sixteen, and Dad had tickets for Disneyland Paris. We had fifteen minutes to change and pack and then we were off and in Paris by midnight. It was fantastic. But when I think back now I remember me and Veeve having a moan in the hotel because it was only Paris and not Florida. It makes me squirm to think how ungrateful we were. We all took Dad and his money for granted. Look how it ended up. Some fairy story.

"Why didn't you tell us you didn't have any money? We could have helped. We're your family. We didn't need all those things. We wouldn't have minded. Why didn't you trust us, Dad?"

I stop and my voice is all choked up. Dad doesn't say anything either. Maybe he's thinking we would have minded.

But then he says, "You know what Nana Hat always says? What doesn't kill you makes you strong."

"This is supposed to be GOOD for us?" I can almost see red in front of my eyes. "You knew how ill I was this year. I thought I was going to die...."

"I know," he cuts in.

"No you don't!" I shout. Then I lower my voice; I don't want everyone to hear my business. "Monica Jones in the bed opposite was talking and laughing one day, and then a few days later she was dead. Remember?"

He nods.

"I thought that was going to happen to me."

Dad flinches but I'm not finished yet. I lean forward and hiss, "I thought *nothing* could be worse than facing your own death at fifteen. Then I saw you steal the money from those wallets. That was a million times worse! And don't get me started on seeing Vee...." My voice breaks down and the tears start.

Dad runs his hand through his hair and stares down the street as I try to control my sobs.

Then he says in a quiet voice, "I'm sorry, Jessie. I'm so

sorry. I can't believe what I did to you; I know I was wrong, so wrong. I should never have asked you to lie for me. I was weak and stupid. I betrayed you; you should be able to trust your Dad. I don't know if I can ever make it up to you."

"Why did you lie, Dad? Why?"

Dad shakes his head. "I've gone over and over it in my head. I should have come clean to your Mum. But it all happened so quickly, the firm crashing, the money drying up. I panicked, went into a spin. All I ever wanted was to be the big man, rich, successful. Nana Hat will tell you. I wanted to give my family what I never had. I didn't want you to suffer the way I did as a kid. In the end I made things worse for you all. I was so stupid, so utterly stupid."

"I'm so ashamed of you, Dad."

"I know."

"You could go to prison if they find out you pinched money from those wallets."

"They have."

"What?"

"I told them. I went round to each one and explained and gave them back the money last week."

"Were they angry?" I can't believe he's done that.

"Let's say I lost a few good friends, but my conscience is clear."

"Oh." That must have taken some bottle, I think. They were probably really horrible to him. I would have been terrified.

Then I have an awful thought. "What about Anthony Perrins, your partner? You stole his credit card and took his money; he's not going to forgive you. You'll go to prison!"

Veeve'll never get over this, I think, and Mum. This is *never* going to get better.

Dad's head ducks again and I think I might as well go back to work. We're done here.

But then he raises his head and looks me in the eye and says, "That was one of the worst days. I already had debts before things went wrong. But we always had such big bonuses, I wasn't worried. But then the company crashed and Anthony couldn't bail us out anymore. And that day the bank wrote and said they were going to repossess the house; they froze all our accounts. My whole life fell apart in a few short months. I couldn't pay the mortgage or the bills. I didn't even have enough change in my pocket for your dinner money, Jessie."

"Why didn't you tell Mum?"

"I thought she'd leave me."

Neither of us say anything. My parents are going to get divorced, I think, as if things could get any worse.

"That day I couldn't get Anthony's credit card to work and you caught me at the cash machine in the garage, I wasn't in my right mind. You fell over, Jess, didn't you?"

I reach up to my face, there's still a mark there. "You pushed me because I grabbed the card. I hit the wall. You just left me there."

Dad's eyes fill with tears and I don't know which way to look. It's so embarrassing. And yet, at least he feels something, sad, or upset, or sorry. Something is better than the nothing I saw in his eyes that day at the cash machine.

"Everything's a blur about that day. Things were about the worst they could be," he says. "I had a pile of threats from debt collectors and they'd even come to the house when you were all out the week before. I didn't answer the door but I knew they'd be back."

Of course; the bailiffs told us they'd been to the house looking for him.

"You coward!" I blurt out.

Dad covers his eyes with his hand. But he goes on talking. "You're right Jess, of course you are. I was so terrified you saw me and so ashamed. All I could think was, I have to get away. I remember going over the bridge to the pub. There were some of the chaps there from the Marina, celebrating someone's birthday. They gave me a skinful of whisky. I don't know what happened after that, but I woke up on the beach. It was dark and I nearly froze to death. Might have been better if I had died that night."

"No!" Whatever Dad's done to us, I don't want that.

He reaches out and puts his hand on my arm. I let him. It feels warm and comforting.

"I went round to Anthony's and gave him back the card. I hadn't taken any money. He understood. He knew he'd stuffed up; he's lost a lot too – had to sell his holiday home in France and his boat. His wife's taken his kids and gone to live with her sister in Los Angeles."

"You know, you always said I was hungry for money, Dad?" He nods and looks down again. "Well, you made me like that."

I feel so sad standing in the street with my Dad looking like someone has taken him down. Then I say in a quiet voice, "I don't want money anymore. Look what it's done to our family."

Dad doesn't say anything and I wonder if I mean it. I keep wishing I had enough money for a lottery ticket so that we could have a big win and get out of this mess. But saying it out loud has made me realise I don't want to go back to the way we were living before, even if all our money does come back. Which it won't.

"Mum and Veeve are so lucky to have you, eh, Jessie." I frown and look away. Is he mocking me? "I mean it. You were so ill and you got through that and I think it's made you strong, made you a special person. I'm proud of you, Jessie. Very proud."

I can't help it. A glow goes through me. Because he's right, isn't he? I haven't really had time to think about what's happened since the bailiffs came. But I was the one who got us away and into town, got us to Social Services, got that horrible flat. I even got a job before Mum did. It's like I had to be the grown-up, with Veeve having her breakdown and Mum so helpless.

"That's my girl," he says and he reaches out for my hand. But something snaps in me and I whip it away.

"You lied," I say in a low voice, and somehow, because I don't shout it, I can feel how deep it stabs him. All the pain and bitterness and suffering he's caused us in the past few weeks, all the lying and the injury, even pushing me and hurting me. "How could you do it to us? We're your family. I was going to go to Africa with Ryan to run away from it all."

Dad's face crinkles into a little smile and I must admit when I say it out loud it does sound funny. I can't help smiling back.

"No, Jess, whoever this Ryan lad is, I'm sure he's a nice boy, but you're not going to Africa. I'm your Dad and I've come back to look after you all."

He fixes me with his eyes and for a minute he seems like good old Dad again, concerned and being the grown-up, and I just want to sink back into our old life.

But then I shake myself back into reality. There is no old life waiting out there for us, it's all over. Dad has destroyed everything.

"My life is nothing to do with you anymore. Do you have any idea what we've been through, where we live now?"

"I know I've put you all through absolute hell," he says quietly. "I ran away like a coward. I convinced myself that if I disappeared the debt collectors would leave you alone until I could work something out."

"How could you be so stupid!" I yell at him and two blokes in paint-stained overalls turn and look at us from the other side of the street. "Of course they would still come after us, they didn't care that you had disappeared, they wanted their money and so they took the house and the furniture and my laptop and all Veeve's stuff and Mum's Toyota and everything which ever made our lives feel safe. Not like now. We've got no money, no clothes, we live in a leaky, dirty flat and the wind blows straight through the walls. Veeve's taken an overdose and nearly died and she's in hospital and when she comes out, there's NOTHING for her! I work as a dish washer and WE HAVEN'T GOT ANYTHING BECAUSE OF YOU!!"

I break into great, gushing sobs, my chest heaving and heaving and I feel as though I'm going to break into a million pieces. I cover my face with my hands and I just want to run away. Then Dad wraps his arms around me and he hugs me like I've been longing for him to do ever since I saw him take the money from the wallets.

"Of course you're right, Jessie, and it looks like we've both had to learn the hard way, but running away gets you nowhere. I'm back now and I promise you I'll make it up to you and to the whole family."

"Even Nana Hat?" I sob.

"Especially Nana Hat," he says, and for the first time since this all started, I let myself go and I lean against him.

I still don't know if I can trust him, but right now I just want a hug.

Chapter 31

Dad wants to go straight over to the hospital to see Veeve.

I get into his taxi and pull my seatbelt on.

"Let me go in first, OK? I think Mum will be there."

"No, Jess, I'll go in with you. It's my job to face her and tell her the truth," he says, and as we drive off he taps the steering wheel. "Anthony Perrins put in a good word for me with the owner of the cab firm. He feels he owes me, wants to help me get back on my feet."

"Well, *he* hasn't lost everything," I say with a snort.

I feel quite pleased when we cruise past the restaurant and I see the manager glaring out the window. I told him my Mum's sick and I have to go home. He made a big fuss about being short-staffed but in the end he gave me a tenner for the two hours scrubbing I've already done this morning and agreed to keep me on the rota.

I don't know if we can trust Dad. He might lose his job next week, or disappear again. I mean, he owes a lot of money, doesn't he?

We drive past all the shops; there are Christmas decorations everywhere. What will this Christmas be like? Mum and Dad have always taken us out on Christmas morning to the Clubhouse for drinks and mince pies with the girls and their husbands and kids. Sarah and her family always come along as well.

I haven't seen Sar for so long. Will she still want to be friends?

"The first thing I did when I made some money," Dad says, breaking into my thoughts, "was pay back everyone I stole from that Sunday. I couldn't face my family again with that hanging over my head."

"I told Mum and Veeve about the wallets."

He gives me such an agonised look.

"I had to when the bailiffs came, they just didn't understand."

"I really landed you in it, Jessie. But we're a team now."

A team? I'm not sure about that.

"I'll put things right for your Mum and Veeve, OK?"

I shrug. We'll see.

"We didn't go to Florida this year," I say. "And you didn't do the form for the ski trip. You've known for so long." It's like filling in the blanks in a crossword.

Dad nods, "And I couldn't get you all the presents you asked for when you were sick, either."

The memory makes me go red with embarrassment. I was such a spoilt cow, milking Dad for everything I could.

"Sorry, Dad. I was so immature."

He gives a short loud laugh. "You've got nothing to be sorry for, Jess. I was the adult, you were the kid. I made you that way; I encouraged you and Veeve to see me as a bank account."

The hospital is on the edge of town. Dad parks in the car park and I take him up to the ward. I can hear Mum's voice speaking to the nurse as we round the corner to the nurse's station. Mum looks up and sees Dad. Then she lets out this long wail. She goes on and on and I think she's never going to stop. I want the floor to swallow me up.

The nurse stands there staring at us and Dad comes up and says, "Sorry, darling, sorry, I'm so sorry."

I can't stand it any longer and so I pull Mum into the visitor's room, which thankfully is empty, and Dad follows, closing the door behind him.

We all stand there, Mum wailing and Dad dragging a hand through his hair.

Do something! I want to scream at him and then suddenly the door opens. It's Veeve. Oh God!

Mum stops in her tracks, her mouth still open.

Dad cries out, "My darling!" and rushes towards Veeve. But just as he's about to hug her, Veeve throws her arms over her face and lets out a short sharp scream. It sounds like someone has kicked a dog. It's horrible.

Dad stops a few centimetres from Veeve and looks round at me, a totally helpless look on his face. Should I tell him to go? Why doesn't Mum do something? This can't be good for Veeve.

I'm just about to take Veeve out of the room and give up on parents forever when Mum pulls a tissue out of her pocket, wipes her face and says in something like her old commanding voice, "Everyone sit down." No one moves. "Now!" she hollers.

We all jump into action and shuffle around the room until me, Veeve and Mum are sitting together in a group of chairs and Dad is sitting on his own on the other side. That feels about right.

"We're waiting, Ronny," says Mum. Her voice is still wobbling but she's keeping under control.

If Veeve wasn't here I'm pretty sure she'd be yelling at Dad and throwing things by now. I wouldn't blame her either but Veeve's got this sort of shocked look on her face.

Dad starts to tell his story, just like he told me, and we all listen and he winds up with, "And now I've declared myself bankrupt. I won't have any debts anymore."

He stops and looks at Mum.

She's gripping the arms of her chair so hard, her knuckles are white. "How could you? You think everything is OK now, just because *you* don't have any debts...?"

"No, of course not, but...."

"Look what you've done to this family! You've destroyed us, Veeve in hospital, Jess out of school...."

"Why aren't you going to school?" says Dad.

"What's that to you?" I snarl back, and I can feel Veeve flinch by my side. This must be awful for her.

"Shall I take you back to your room?" I offer, but she doesn't answer.

"See," says Mum. "Veeve hasn't spoken a word since all this. Look at the state of her."

"But you must understand, all of you," Dad says, looking round at us. "I had to go away to get everything sorted out."

"What we needed was *you* no matter what was happening. You ran away and left us to it, you...."

"Mum!"

We all turn in shock. It's Veeve. She's spoken. I want to

leap up and grab her and hug her but I'm afraid to move.

"Dad," says Veeve, and a tear rolls down her cheek, "I missed you."

Veeve gets up like a little ghost in her white dressing gown, with her face all thin and pale. She walks slowly across the room and stands in front of Dad.

For a second I think he's going to do nothing and Veeve will collapse or maybe even fall down dead. But just as I open my mouth to scream at Dad to save her, he stands up and takes her in his arms and rocks her.

Mum and me sit and stare, and while we are all silent Dad starts to speak in a quiet voice, "It's all going to be all right now, Veeve, I promise. Dad's here and I'm going to take care of everything."

I feel tears well up again. I look over at Mum. Her face is very pale and her mouth is set in a grim line, like she's gritting her teeth really hard.

"My new boss has a holiday home near the ferry," Dad's saying, "around the Kench, where the old houseboats are. He's been looking for someone to take it over for the winter, doesn't like it to stay empty. He trusts me because Anthony recommended me for the job."

That word - trust. It's such a big word when you think about it. Dad broke our trust, betrayed us all but Anthony Perrins trusts him enough to recommend him. I've been left feeling no one is loyal anymore. Dad, Ryan – even Veeve – disappeared. But whose fault is it? Everyone has their reasons and mostly they are good reasons. Mum hasn't let

223

me down and neither has Nana Hat. So maybe I have to put that big word trust back into use again and not feel like it's gone forever.

Mum gives a little shake of her head and says, "Do you have any idea where we've been living? Drunks going past the door all hours and the roof leaking. When those bailiffs came I thought I was going to collapse. It was Jessica who pulled us out of that horrendous situation and got us all to town. Where were you when we needed you! Eh?"

So Mum doesn't know if she can trust Dad either, and somehow that feels OK. Why should she, just because he chooses to walk back into our lives today?

"I'm so sorry, darling. I can't imagine what it's been like. When I went off I thought it was for the best. I thought you only needed me when I was earning money, and I'd failed hadn't I? But I'm back now and I promise that I'll...."

"No, Ronny," Mum cuts in.

I think she's going to tell him to leave. I suddenly realise I couldn't bear it if he left again even after everything he's done. We've only just got him back and I can't help the way I feel, can I?

Mum stands up and walks over to the window. She's got her back to us but there's something in the line of her shoulders that feels different. She looks out of the window for a minute and then she turns and says again, "No, Ronny."

I stand up to protest.

"Sit down, Jess," Mum snaps at me.

I raise my eyebrows at her but she doesn't respond so I sit back down again.

Mum starts to speak again. "It's time for things to change in this family."

She pauses and there's a new tone in her voice, stronger, more as though *she's* in charge. Like when I was sick and she took over as Florence Mum.

Then she goes on, "From now on we are going to do everything together – we're all going to pull our weight, well, as far as we can." She gives Veeve a little smile. "But no longer do we expect Dad to carry all the burden for the rest of us, right girls?"

I'm not sure I get it, and give Mum a frown.

"Don't you see?" she says. "This isn't all your Dad's fault. I'm as much to blame as him, spending our money and never taking an interest in how much we really had. "

"We were as bad," I say and I look at Veeve. She gives a tiny nod.

"So if we're going to be a family again," Mum goes on, "we rely on each other and not just on one person. Agreed?"

"Agreed," I say, and a flood of relief goes through me. All I have to do is be sixteen-year-old Jess again. Finally.

Then Veeve speaks up, "But Dad has to stay."

"Is that what everyone wants?" asks Dad.

Me and Veeve look at Mum and then we all three nod.

"So tell us about this house on the Kench," says Mum.

Her face is still quite grim but she looks ready to take on the world.

Dad's face clears and he says, "It's quite small, but very nice, newly decorated, new kitchen, the lot. It's even got a dishwasher."

Me and mum exchange approving nods.

"It's only got two bedrooms; the girls will have to share, but we'll give them the biggest room, put desks in, everything they need."

"What's the point? I'm not going back to school, I've got a job," I mutter.

"You and Veeve are both going back to school, Jessica," says Mum.

"Of course you are," says Dad. "I want you to get a proper education and do something useful with your lives. Not make the mess I made."

If he really means it then maybe things will be OK. I really hope so because if Dad betrays us a second time there'll be nothing left.

"Well, that's agreed then," says Mum. "You'd better show us this place. I don't think I can stand that leaky roof for one more night."

Chapter 32
Jess and Ryan

dec 22

Three days to Christmas and Dad's already given us our present. A laptop and broadband. The laptop is second-hand from someone at Dad's work, and we've only got mobile broadband, so it cuts out quite often. But it's BRILLIANT!!!

It's early morning and I'm sitting up in bed writing my diary; I'm using a torch so I don't wake Veeve. She only came home two days ago. She still doesn't speak very much, and she has to see a doctor every week, but when we're in bed at night we whisper to each other about everything that's happened and how frightened we've both been. She keeps saying how sorry she is she took the pills and scared me half to death.

"We're sisters," she said to me the first night. "You were so strong when all this happened. I'll never forget that."

It made me glow inside.

We still squabble, of course. Veeve's drawn up this huge, complicated rota for turns on the computer, with six different felt tip pens. It's mad.

I started to cross out bits of it and we had a screaming match. But we made up. "It's OK to fight," says Veeve. "We're survivors."

Miriam Halahmy

Mum and Dad are not getting divorced. Relief. I know they're not the same but hopefully it'll get better.

Veeve says that whatever Dad did, he's trying to put it right and we do love him. That's why we took him back. She's right. Part of me is still angry with him though.

Being closer to my sister makes me think of Ryan and James, and how they were together after the climbing accident. The rest of us could have disappeared for all they cared. They were stuck to each other like glue.

I was so jealous. I didn't think me and Veeve could ever be like that.

But we are, finally, and it's great.

The most weird thing – Ryan found me on Facebook!!??? I accepted him and he messaged to meet up. He's coming to the chip shop at two today. Can't help feeling a tiny bit excited.

Me and Mum and Dad went to see Nana Hat last week. Veeve wasn't well enough to come with us. Dad sat there with his head dropped almost in his lap and told Nana everything. She already knew most of it from Mum, but she just sat there, her shawl over her knees, nodding away, her white hair bobbing up and down on her forehead.

Then she leaned forward, patted his hand and said, "I'm proud of you, Ronny."

Proud! I nearly choked.

But then she said, "Mother always said it didn't do no good hiding away. You got to face your demons. You came back to put things right, Ronny. Good lad."

"We'll see," said Mum. "He's on probation for now."

But I've seen them have a cuddle now and then and I think they'll be OK.

I've still got a job. I couldn't face going back to the restaurant; my new job is in the chip shop on Saturdays. I'm never going to rely on Dad for all my money again. Mum works in the salon three days a week. I think she feels the same but I think she kind of likes it as well. Dad still drives his taxi.

Sar's been amazing.

"I'm not friends with you for your money, Jess, babes," she said.

She loves our little house. We go for long walks on the beach and talk and talk. She's caught me up with all the gossip. I'm actually looking forward to school next term.

My shift starts at ten so I have breakfast in our little kitchen. It's bright and clean, no leaks and no horrible dog waiting for me outside. Bliss. Dad's already left in his taxi and we all agreed Veeve should sleep as much as she wants.

Then I walk to the bus stop. By lunchtime the shop is really busy. I'm serving a young couple with a baby when I see Ryan standing quietly in the corner by the door. He's five minutes early. He's wearing a padded jacket and he's cut his hair short but not too short. He's still got those wiry curls. He looks much more grown-up than I remember and I feel a bit shy. Maybe this wasn't a good idea after all. I don't need any more trouble in my life like a broken heart. Again.

Scott comes into the chip shop sometimes with Paige Butcher. They're all over each other in front of me.

I asked Dad about the Gina Butcher affair again.

"I didn't do anything, Jessie, I promise you. Money got moved around between accounts, there was a big deal on at the time, it was a genuine error and Gina Butcher took against me over it."

I believe him. Dad let us down, big time, but now we're all moving on and we have to put the past behind us.

"Ready?" Ryan asks me as I wipe my hands on a tea towel.

I nod and say, "Just a minute."

I go out the back to the stock cupboard and pull on my coat. I check my phone and there's a message from Mum saying she's cooking spaghetti tonight and can I pick up a tin of tomatoes. She ends it with XOX. Kiss hug kiss.

We hug a lot these days. That's one of the best things.

Mum's friends all seem to have disappeared now she doesn't go to the Clubhouse anymore, except Angela.

"Loyal little Angela," Mum says with a smile.

They've been friends since school. They go to a knitting circle now in the community hall. I've been along, too. It's quite nice sitting with the women and listening to them gossip. They're nicer than the girls and Mum seems at home with them. I like knitting, it's peaceful and warm and you can make some really cool stuff. I'm going to start a sweater in the New Year. Sar thinks I'm mad but then I nearly did go mad so I don't mind.

"Beach?" I say to Ryan when I go out front. He nods and we walk off together.

It's a beautiful day, not too cold. The yachts are zipping about over the water between Hayling Island and the Isle of Wight and the sea is very calm. The waves are breaking in tiny ripples along the shore and the tide is out so there's a stretch of sand uncovered.

"I tried to find you," Ryan starts up. "Went to the house and saw the shutters."

"Dad lost the house; the bailiffs came and threw us out."

"Max told me."

We're silent again. So much has happened since we were last together. That stupid weekend climbing, the accident, Ryan telling me about the baby, me not telling him about all the stuff Dad had been up to. I don't know what to say to him. But I feel his body loping along next to mine and I feel drawn towards him like a magnet.

"Look Jess, I really wanted to see you again. But if you...."

"No, I mean, yes, me too."

He moves closer and I feel his hand slip into mine. It feels so good.

Suddenly I can't really remember why we stopped seeing each other. He said he didn't even love that other girl. Having a baby, that's such a huge thing. When Ryan first told me I felt overwhelmed.

But I've been thinking about it again recently and the fact is, life's too short to worry about everything that happens. After all the things I've been through with my illness and then watching Dad steal, standing up to the bailiffs and working in that awful kitchen, and even looking after Mum and Veeve, surely I can take a chance with Ryan again.

I'm going for the Severe, I tell myself. I'm jamming my fingers in the cracks and heading to the top. If I fall – well, I'll get back up again.

I stop and pull Ryan round to face me.

"Let's start again," I say.

There's a flicker of happiness in his eyes and he doesn't say no.

I stare out over his shoulder at the Solent. The water is a deep blue under the Christmas sun. If it wasn't so cold you could almost imagine you were on a beach in Spain.

Then I take a deep breath, force a smile on my face and go for it.

"Hey," I say, "I'm Jess Jayne, biggest flirt in Year 11, leader of the Jayne gang, meanest girl gang in school."

Ryan's face creases into a frown.

Then I say, "Only I'm not that girl anymore. I'm Jessica Fitzgerald. I'm sixteen years old, I work in a chip shop and I just want to be with you."

"Hey," he says and I can't help smiling a bit. "I'm Ryan John O'Neill. I'm training to be a mechanic, I want to learn how to fix engines and I'm going to be a Dad."

His eyes are full of sadness and hope and they're gleaming with unshed tears.

I reach into the plastic bag I'm carrying and pull out a little pair of knitted baby booties. "I know," I say. "I made these for the baby."

That makes him laugh out loud and he drags a sleeve across his eyes. When he looks at me, his face is crinkled in a smile. A good smile.

I smile back and lean my chin forward. Our lips are almost touching, our eyes locked, unblinking.

"Jess...."

"No, I'm Jessica now."

"Jessica," he corrects himself, carefully. "Are we going to be OK?"

"We're going to be perfect," I say.

Then he kisses me full on the lips and the moment lasts forever.

ENDS

About Miriam Halahmy

 Miriam Halahmy has published novels, short stories and poetry for adults and young people. Her stories and poems have been included in anthologies, read on the radio and performed on stage. Her novels are constructed around strong characters and real-life situations. Miriam believes that teenage relationships should be treated with respect, by both adults and young people.

A Londoner all her life, Miriam's family lived on Hayling Island for twenty-five years and she has been visiting the Island regularly since the 1970s. She decided to set her novels there because of its beauty and mystery. Her favourite time on Hayling is the winter when the Island is at its most peaceful.

Miriam continues to write and publish poetry, articles and book reviews. She has completed her cycle of three novels set on Hayling Island and is writing further novels about young adults who are dealing with real-life situations, including love and loss.

www.miriamhalahmy.com

Acknowledgements

Many thanks to those trustworthy and supportive fellow writers who commented on drafts of this novel, to my editor, Lucy Cuthew, and to everyone at Albury Books.

A particular thanks to the climbing community, especially Cole Styron, Richard Hogan and Mark 'Zippy' Pretty, who gave me such valuable advice on rock climbing and scenarios for the accident. Any errors in the narrative are down to me.

As a student I climbed regularly on the gritstone edges of Staffordshire and suffered my own fall, like most climbers. Climbing is about defying gravity and I have to admit I still miss it.

For always making me feel so welcome, a big thanks to the Hayling Islanders, many of whom have commented enthusiastically on my previous two Hayling novels, Hidden and Illegal. I hope you will also enjoy this concluding novel in the Hayling cycle.

All three of the books in this cycle which spans four years of my writing career have been supported, commented upon and read carefully by my husband, Rafael, who remains my rock on the sometimes severe climb through life.